Tomorrow's Blessings

Blueberry Beach Novels, Volume 2

Jessie Gussman

Published by Jessie Gussman, 2021.

This is a work of fiction. Similarities to real people, places, or events are entirely coincidental.

TOMORROW'S BLESSINGS

First edition. March 21, 2021.

Written by Jessie Gussman.

Cover art by Julia Gussman
Editing by Heather Hayden[1]
Narration by Jay Dyess[2]

CLICK HERE[3] if you'd like to subscribe to my newsletter and find out why people say "Jessie's is the only newsletter I open and read." And "You make my day brighter. Love, love, love reading your newsletters. I don't know where you find time to write books. You are so busy living life. A true blessing."

1. **https://hhaydeneditor.com/**
2. **https://www.acx.com/narrator?p=A3VWKVSC6MFZHW**
3. https://BookHip.com/FASFD

Chapter 1

THE SUN WAS DYING.

At least it was going out in a blaze of glory.

Clichés, but Anitra knew exactly why someone had looked at the sunset and thought those words.

Probably, they'd just gotten word that their son who had been fighting leukemia for the last three years was out of remission.

Probably, they'd been told there was nothing except experimental treatments left, and none of those held much hope or promise.

Probably, they'd been working their fingers to the bone, trying to take care of their business, along with being a mom to the son who just wanted to be a normal kid, and still pay their bills, while their deadbeat ex kept haranguing them for a divorce, which they were loath to give, because it might mess up their health insurance.

Probably, if someone lived a life like that, when they looked at the sunset, instead of seeing the beauty and the uniqueness that each and every one was, they would see it as death.

Anitra Pollard stood on the shore of Lake Michigan, the breeze across the lake blowing the tunic dress she wore as well as her hair. It was a little chilly but felt warm after the subzero temperatures that blew off the lake in December and January.

Her soul cried out to the Lord, begging for the life of her son, even though she knew it was futile.

She'd been hoping for a miracle for three years.

Hoping that when Jordan had been declared to be in remission, that was a bit of the miracle she'd been begging for.

No such luck.

All spring, Jordan had been talking about angels in heaven, and she'd allowed him to do so, of course, but it scared her too.

A premonition on her part, or more likely his.

He seemed eager to go.

That made it easier, in a way.

But it wasn't in her DNA, as a mother especially, to stop fighting.

To pry her fingers up and let go.

She wanted to shake her fist at the sunset, angry that God could make something so beautiful while her life contained so much pain.

They would fight this new diagnosis, of course. And that would mean more trips to Chicago, more loss of sleep, and more feeling overwhelmed as she did it all as a single mother.

Despite the fact that her divorce was not final.

The pier on her right, long and little more than a dark shadow as the sun crept lower, almost disappearing, grounded her somewhat.

As long as she had lived in Blueberry Beach, all of her thirty-three years, the pier had been there, along with the lake, reflecting each sunset.

Solid, weathering every storm.

The pier wasn't particularly pleasant to look at, but it felt stable, when nothing else in her life seemed to be anymore.

She supposed everyone was looking for stability.

Maybe God typically provided that.

But lately, it seemed like God had just upended her life time after time.

Half the time, she wondered if He was even there.

Although she couldn't exactly look at the expanse of the lake before her and truly believe He wasn't.

She carried her sandals. Her feet were bare, cool in the sand.

She hadn't been gone long, but Iva May, who came to watch her son for an hour or so every night while she took a walk, wouldn't mind going home early.

It was cool enough and early enough in the season that the beach was deserted.

Mostly deserted. She passed a man.

A tourist, since she didn't recognize him.

She supposed he was athletic and strong, although her head was in such a state that she didn't pay attention.

The idea of noticing a man felt strange. She was still married. Soon to be divorced. It was just a matter of getting the papers and signing them.

And then trying to figure out how that affected the health insurance she needed for Jordan, which is why she'd been dragging her feet to begin with. Her marriage had ended a long time ago when her husband had found someone else.

Overwhelmed, but too restless to continue to stay and look at the water that often calmed her, especially this time of evening, she whirled, intent on her normal business walk, heading back to her small shop and the second floor apartment that she lived in over it with her son.

Maybe it was everything that was happening.

Maybe it was because she hadn't eaten all day, fasting and praying because she knew God was listening, He just wasn't giving her the answer she craved, or maybe she was just getting old.

Whatever it was, she whirled too quickly, and the earth tilted around her, going fuzzy, then black, then she was on the sand, its wetness digging into her cheek, the cool roughness feeling good, if odd, against her hot skin.

Things seemed to darken then lighten and then blacken again.

She didn't feel any particular hurry to get up, not even when a large wave touched her toes, reminding her that Lake Michigan was beautiful, wild, and very, very cold in March.

"Are you okay?" A voice, strong, low, and full of compassion, seemed to warm her the whole way to her cold toes.

She didn't recognize it, although it seemed a little familiar.

Maybe a tourist who had been in her diner. She wasn't sure.

A hand settled on her shoulder, and she gave in to the pressure, rolling until she lay on her back.

"Ma'am? Can you hear me?"

She could. She supposed she should let him know. She was bothered by something. What was the thing?

The hand, strong and warm, shook her again. "Your eyes are open. Your pupils responsive. Are you deliberately not answering me? Are you deaf?"

The last question wasn't made sarcastically. It was like he was sincerely asking if she were deaf.

"I'm fine," she whispered, knowing she was anything but. Of course, the problems that she had weren't anything the man thought they might be, but he didn't know that.

She was tempted, for the first time ever, to just get up and walk into the water. Keep walking until it was over her head and she disappeared.

Even if she disappeared, her problems wouldn't; she just wouldn't be here to solve them anymore.

They'd disappear for her, but she'd leave behind bigger problems for her son and her friends or whoever took her son, since her ex was highly unlikely to.

"I'm going to call an ambulance," the man finally said.

"Please don't. Please," she whispered.

"Sit up and talk to me, and I won't."

She didn't want to sit up. She wanted to just lie on the sand and let it take her. Or rest, or just bury her problems with something. Lake

Michigan seemed as good of a something as anything. But since the man had been kind enough to stop and try to do a good deed, she didn't want to punish him.

No good deed goes unpunished ran through her head, and she almost laughed.

She believed it. Had lived it most of her life.

Being good and doing the right thing hadn't seemed to pay off for her.

At least not where Jordan or her marriage or her personal life was concerned.

She pushed up, slowly, the big warm hand behind her pushing, helping, and steadying her as she made it upright and bent her legs, pulling her knees up to her chest and wrapping her arms around them.

Putting her head down in a position she held often as a young girl, sitting on the edge of the lake.

It seemed like forever ago. She would like to be over her problems and not be burdened. Just for a little bit.

"You still don't seem like you're quite all there." The man dropped from his crouch to sit beside her, his position imitating hers to some extent but keeping one hand on her back, steadying her.

She could have told him she didn't need it, but forgive her, she was just savoring the touch of someone strong and capable, even if he couldn't share the problems that were in her head.

He sat close, and she wasn't sure whether it was her or him, but when she lifted her head, it ended up on his shoulder.

It didn't keep her warm, but it did feel good.

It had been years since her husband had offered any kind of support.

She'd been alone so long.

"Do you often walk on the beach?" the man asked.

She shook her head no, then she looked at him. He wasn't bad to look at. With a strong jaw and kind eyes. A straight nose.

She couldn't see much else because of the fading light, and she supposed she didn't need to.

She was pretty sure he had been in her shop earlier that day, but it didn't surprise her that he didn't recognize her.

People who came in the diner often didn't since she had her hair pulled back severely in a bun and usually wore her reading glasses perched on the end of her nose. Not to mention, she did a lot of the cooking, and Iva May usually worked the cash register.

It didn't matter about tourists anyway. They were here one week and gone the next.

She enjoyed them, normally. Although the last three years had been a trial.

The man was still looking at her. It made her feel like he truly cared.

"I just had some really bad news today. I suppose, when you get bad news after bad news after bad news, it gets harder with each blow to bounce back. Maybe that was it. I don't know."

"Did you eat anything today?"

"No."

"Did you drink anything?"

Maybe. Yes? No... She really couldn't remember. "I think I had coffee this morning."

"Maybe you should try to take care of yourself. That might have something to do with it."

She nodded. "You're right."

His advice, delivered in a tone that said he cared for her, despite not knowing her, was well meant. She wanted to soak it up, as impossible as it was.

How was she supposed to explain to him that she could hardly take care of herself when she had a son who was dying of cancer, and a business to run so that she could continue to pay her bills, and a husband who'd been gone longer than he'd been with her and wanted a divorce so he could marry—not the woman he left her for—but the next woman or the next. She couldn't even keep track. It was one of them.

That she was afraid her health insurance would disappear when she signed her divorce papers, and she wouldn't be able to make a living if she had to be in the hospital with her son and couldn't work in her diner.

She couldn't explain all that to a stranger.

She allowed her head to continue to rest on his shoulder. It should have felt weird, but it didn't. It felt good, like someone else was beside her. For once.

"Thank you. Thank you for just sitting here with your arm around me."

He didn't say anything for a bit, like maybe he found their position odd but right as well, and then he said, "You're welcome. It seems like maybe you need it."

She nodded, moving her head up and down on his shoulder. "I think I do."

His left hand reached over his body and touched hers which rested on her knee. He touched the ring finger where her wedding band had sat for years. She'd taken it off when her husband had informed her that he was moving in with someone else, which was not quite a year before her son had been diagnosed with cancer.

She noticed, as his hand settled over hers, that he wasn't wearing a ring either.

A thought tumbled around in her brain, as rhythmic as the sound of the waves lapping the shore, as the wide-open lake breeze, fresh and clean, washed over them.

What was the point of doing right? She was tired of being good. Tired of doing everything perfectly—as perfectly as she could. Tired of being the responsible one. Tired of being the one who made sure things got done. Tired of always shouldering the load and picking up the slack.

She was tired. Tired of no one ever seeing her, appreciating her, tired of always doing everything for everyone else. Tired of being the one everyone depended on. Tired. Tired. Tired.

Normally, she would never sit on the bank of the lake in the arms of a man whose name she didn't even know.

She'd certainly never done anything like that before.

She wasn't interested in tourists anyway. They were here for a bit and then gone.

Growing up in Blueberry Beach, she'd learned she couldn't form a lasting relationship with someone like that.

But maybe that's what she needed. Something transient. After all, if she were going to do something she knew to be wrong, who better to do it with than a stranger?

Don't be ridiculous. No one needs that.

The voice of reason in her head had always been loud and strong. She was tired of listening to it.

Look where it had gotten her. Soon to be single, having been essentially a single mom for years anyway. Responsible for all the bills from the last bout of cancer, heart broken by a man who couldn't keep his promises. And now her son was going to be taken from her.

It sure didn't seem like she was going to reap what she sowed. Seemed like she'd done nothing but reap hardship all her life.

She shivered. The man's arm tightened around her.

The hand that was over hers moved slightly down, warming her fingers.

She shifted her hand just a little, and their fingers slid together.

Under her cheek, the man tensed.

That hadn't been his intention. But after five or six heartbeats, he relaxed again, and his other hand slid up and down her arm, warming it.

"Thank you for stopping for me," she said softly.

"Of course. I couldn't walk on by without making sure you were okay."

Of course. He would have stopped for anyone. She knew that.

"Do you live around here?" he asked. "Or are you just visiting too?"

"Can I not say?" she asked, not being coy but truly meaning it. She didn't want to be *her* anymore. Even though she knew a person couldn't just walk away from their life.

Well, her husband could walk away from *his* life and ditch everything, but she couldn't. Not forever.

Maybe she could for an hour.

But no more. She couldn't let herself.

"So you're wanted by the police?" the man asked, and she smiled, wishing she were free to laugh too.

When was the last time she'd been with a man who had been charming and funny? For her.

It seemed like never.

"I am," she said, going along with his statement. "I don't want you to get messed up with my crimes. It's better that you stay an innocent bystander."

The man grunted, his side touching hers, feeling right. "I'm not very good at being a bystander. If something's happening, I guess you can see that I have a tendency to get involved in the thick of it."

She shook her head. "Shh. Don't tell me anything about yourself. I don't want to be able to describe the witness."

"I think you can plead the fifth."

"I suppose I could, but it would be better to be able to tell the truth."

The man gave a low whistle. "An honest person. Those are hard to find nowadays."

"Tell me about it," she said, and she thought about her ex. What she wouldn't do for an honest person. An honest *husband*.

"I guess if we are being honest, but I'm not allowed to give you identifying details, maybe I can still say I don't typically sit on the beach with my arm around women that I don't know."

"I've never done this."

"Hmm. So you're not from around here." His voice held humor. "Be careful. I'll figure you out yet."

She smiled, not the slightest bit tempted to tell him that she'd lived beside Lake Michigan her whole life.

"Is this your first time in Blueberry Beach?" she asked, referring to her hometown, although the man didn't know it.

"No. I've been here several times. My job, which I'm not allowed to tell you about, and the training that I've done for it, which I'm *really* not allowed to tell you about, has taken up a lot of my time. And now, I'm at a bit of a crossroads, and I took a week off to come here and make a decision."

She grunted. "What is it about the water, and the vastness of it stretching out in front of you, that makes you feel small and almost insignificant, and it puts your problems in perspective?"

At least, sometimes it did. Even as she said it, she knew it wasn't true for her. Not lately. But she knew the feeling, because normal problems looked small against the water and the vastness it contained. "Maybe that makes it easier to make a decision, when you feel like it's not life or death in the universe."

"I hadn't thought about it that way. But I can see that you might be right. I just know my thoughts get clear, and things seem to fall into place when I come out here, and watch the sunset, listen to the waves, and feel the slower pace of life. I think this is the way life was meant to be lived."

She could agree with that. But just because one lived in a lakeside town didn't mean a person didn't have problems.

"I think this is the kind of place where tourists," she almost said "like us," but she didn't want to say anything that wasn't true, "go to make idyllic memories that they take home with them to unpack during their mundane lives the rest of the year."

"I think so. You make better memories when you're with someone." He paused, then said lower, "Every time I've come, I've been alone."

He was so gentle, his voice that good mixture of culture and gravel that touched her just right, and she couldn't be the only one. She had trouble believing he was alone.

"After breakups?" she asked.

She'd spent a lot of time at the beach after her husband left. Iva May didn't mind walking across the yard between her small house and Anitra's apartment. She could watch her game shows in the evening on Anitra's TV just as easily as she could watch them on hers.

Not to mention, she seemed to have a few ghosts in her own past that made her sympathetic to Anitra's situation.

"No. Sometimes, life just seems a little overwhelming. Or a lot overwhelming. Me coming here had to do with that job and the training that I was talking about earlier, but I'm not allowed to talk about it, so I won't. Because, in a way, I kind of like the idea." He paused for a bit, and they listened to the water lapping along the shore. The moon had risen above the eastern horizon behind them and shone down, blocked occasionally by clouds.

"The idea of not knowing who you're with?" she asked, and he didn't say anything.

She'd given up that he was going to answer and let her mind wander. It wasn't that she didn't want to know who he was. He seemed like a nice man.

But she didn't have any room in her life for real romance. As much as she might want it, and, with her divorce imminent, as much as she might be able to correct at least one of her many mistakes.

But she just didn't want another entanglement. Didn't want more. Especially not a tourist.

When she was in high school, she'd had a couple short and sweet summer romances.

Nothing more than holding hands and maybe a kiss under the pier.

They'd always promised to write, and sometimes they did. But not for long. Never for long.

She had never been interested in anything like that, but as the mystery man's hand tightened around her arm, she felt like maybe it was okay to sit here with someone she didn't know and had no intentions of ever seeing again.

Regardless, maybe she was crazy, but for the first time in her life, she didn't care about tomorrow. After all, tomorrow always took care of itself.

Chapter 2

DR. JOHN CHAMBERS, pediatric oncologist, sat on the lakeshore with his arm around a woman he didn't know the name of and contemplated how odd life could be sometimes.

His work wasn't exactly happy work, most of the time, and he dealt daily with mothers just like the lady beside him.

He'd learned, probably in the first year that he'd started his specialty, that he couldn't get attached.

He could care, how could he not? But he couldn't get attached.

It hadn't really mattered, because he didn't seem to be the kind of man that women were attracted to.

He wasn't quite sure what kind of man that was, but women seemed to prize cockiness and arrogance. Most of the time when he looked at the men who were married, they seemed to be confident almost to that point.

Part of him had come to the decision that in order for women to see a man as attractive, he had to be a jerk.

Maybe he hadn't met the right woman.

His rigorous training hadn't provided many opportunities to meet women, and he'd been very focused and driven by his work.

But there was something about this woman, something vulnerable yet strong, that appealed to his protective instincts, and now that he knew she was okay, he was enjoying just sitting beside her.

She seemed a little wild, maybe fairy-like, as she stood watching the lake, the wind blowing her dress back in billowing waves, along with her hair which was slightly longer than shoulder length and a pretty brown.

He'd seen her as he walked along the lake toward her, not intending to talk to her, until she'd fallen. He'd jogged the last fifty feet.

Hearing she hadn't eaten all day and wasn't sure whether she'd drunk anything, and then assuming that she had some things on her mind, assured him that it wasn't a medical condition that had caused her collapse.

She just needed a shoulder.

Like so many people did.

She felt good and right under his arm, and when he touched her ring finger, she hadn't said anything. Then he deliberately put his hand over top of hers, so she would know he wasn't doing anything wrong, either.

It seemed like that didn't matter to most people anymore, but it mattered to him.

Even sitting on the beach with his arm around another man's wife wouldn't have sat right.

"I never realized how pretty the moonlight is on the water. I guess once the sun went down, I always went in."

"Oh, it is. You should see it when it's a full moon. Just absolutely gorgeous."

"So you come here a lot?"

She seemed to pause. She was definitely a mystery and wanted to stay that way. "When I can. But I've seen it as the moon sets on the far horizon, and that's gorgeous too. Not like a sunset, but pretty in its own way."

He looked at the water, every ripple reflecting the light of the moon over the top of them, constantly moving and shifting, and he could only imagine how much more interesting it would be reflecting a full moon.

"I'm going to have to revise my initial opinion and decide that you're a local girl if you keep talking like that."

"I think it's more fun to imagine than to actually know."

"I think you might be right." More fun, but easier to find the girl again if he knew her name at least.

"I'll tell you what," he said, reaching into his pocket and pulling out one of his business cards. "It's too dark for you to read this now, but you keep it, and if you want to contact me, my name and number is on it. Don't be intimidated," he added, knowing from experience that some people would be. If he had a card with just his name on it, he would have given her that.

Not his title with "doctor" in front of his name and the name of the department he was over. It looked more intimidating and important than it was.

He was considering leaving that job anyway and taking one that paid less money but gave him more time to have a life.

He wasn't sure why he was even thinking about it, since he didn't really need more time, considering he didn't have a family.

But maybe, he'd seen enough of the shortness of life to know that he wanted a little more from his than what he had.

Before it was too late.

She took the card from him without looking at it, and her hand disappeared to her side before it came back up to hug her knees again.

Her other hand still held onto his, their fingers threaded together, and he didn't mind that at all.

In fact, he kind of liked it. For her, and for him.

"Does that mean that you're ready to leave?" she asked, not moving at all from her spot on the beach.

"No. It means, if you feel so inclined to get in touch with me again, know that I am, too."

He didn't normally talk like that, but maybe he'd not been aggressive enough, and that's why he'd ended up alone. Maybe he needed to take a few more risks in the relationship department than what he had been.

"Do you sail?" he asked, thinking that that wasn't too intrusive of a question, and it might get her talking to him a little.

"I don't. I've been out on boats, but that bug never bit me. Plus, the lake changes so quickly and so rapidly, it's a little scary. I can swim, but I know I can't swim the way I would need to if a boat were to sink."

"I see. I think you *are* a local girl."

She didn't say anything, and he felt bad mentioning it yet again. She hadn't wanted to tell him the first time, and she didn't appreciate him bringing it up again. And again.

He probably only succeeded in making her clam up more.

"I won't mention it again. I guess I feel comfortable with you, in a way that's kind of surprising considering we just met. Not to scare you, but that's rare for me and something worth keeping or, at the very least, spending time examining."

"Not with me," she said with a bit of a sigh. "Trust me, I'm doing you a favor. Life is pretty complicated."

"I guess we make time for the things that are important to us." He'd heard that line a lot over the years, and he'd wondered about it, because he was willing to make time for romance and for a woman, but the opportunity just hadn't presented itself. Not with a woman he'd felt so comfortable with.

Now that he had found something that felt so right, it was a little frustrating that she wasn't willing.

"I guess Blueberry Beach must get its name from all the blueberry farms around the area?"

"It does. The ground in this area is sandy and acidic and perfect for growing blueberries. If you've never been here in the summer—July especially—you should make sure to come. That's when they're ripe, and there are blueberry stands everywhere."

"Blueberries are healthy."

She turned her head and gave him a look. For some reason, he didn't want her to know he was a doctor and all the other trappings that came with what he'd accomplished in his job. He just wanted to be himself for this evening.

So, he leaned a little closer. She froze, and he didn't move until he felt her relax against him, leaning in a little more and brushing his lips across her temple. It certainly wasn't a normal action for him, and from the skittish way she was acting, it wasn't typical for her, either.

Which made him feel, more than ever, that, while he didn't believe in soulmates, they shared something special.

He asked her about the town and the blueberries, and she talked like a knowledgeable local, which didn't surprise him, and he assumed she was from around the area.

He also assumed that he might have the opportunity to see her again. Especially if he made the decision that tonight's chance encounter had made him more inclined to make.

So when she lifted her head and said, "I better go. I have some things I need to do," he was disappointed but not devastated because he'd convinced himself she was from around the area and that he would see her again.

"Do you want me to walk you to your home?" he asked, thinking he probably knew the answer but hoping that it might be different than what he thought.

"No, thank you." She stood to her feet, and he got to his, and they both spent a few moments brushing themselves off.

She faced him, and all he could see was her hair blowing across her face even though he searched as hard as he could to see her eyes. To see some kind of facial feature that he would be able to recognize.

At least he'd recognize her voice.

"I appreciate you sitting with me. It was...nice to have a shoulder to lean on for just a bit. It was even nicer to pretend that it was real. Thank you for letting me have a little dream."

He didn't deal too much in dreams and stuff like that, but he supposed he could if he had a woman who wanted to be beside him.

There wasn't a lot he wouldn't give up because the life he'd made for himself was a lonely life. Even though he was what most people would consider extremely successful.

He'd come to realize he was extremely dissatisfied.

"You won't change your mind about giving me your name at least?" he asked, gently, because he didn't want her to think he was pushing her, but also, he couldn't resist one last try to give him that much more opportunity to find her again.

She shook her head. "It's for the best."

"Don't forget you're holding my card. Use it if you need it."

She nodded. But she did so in such an absentminded way that he was sure that the card was going to stay in her pocket, and she would never read the front of it.

He tried to suppress the disappointment that thought brought to his chest as it deflated. "I'm serious. If I can ever do anything for you, even if you're not sure, let me know."

She looked down at the beach and shuffled her feet. Hope flared in his chest because he thought she might actually be thinking of either giving him her name or asking him to help her with something.

But she finally looked back up at him, and he thought he saw her teeth flash in the moonlight in a little smile as she said, "Thank you again. Bye."

She didn't give him a backward glance but strode with purpose away from the beach and away from him.

Chapter 3

ANITRA WALKED INTO her house, shivering.

Not because she was cold, but because while sitting in that man's arms had been comforting and reassuring, walking away from him had been hard.

When they'd been standing there, and he'd offered, twice, to help her in any way, the only thing she could think of was to ask him to kiss her goodbye.

Which was an absolutely crazy thing, and she didn't know where the thought came from or where she could shove it to pretend she'd never had such a thing enter her mind.

She could know his name by now. Her diner was less than a block from the beach, with her apartment above it taking up all of the second story.

Even though the walk was ten minutes from where she was at the pier, she hadn't pulled his card out of her pocket and didn't plan to look at it.

Tourists were all the same. They loved Blueberry Beach and its people while they were in town, but then they went back to their regular lives, and she never saw or heard from them again.

Of course, her ex-husband had stayed for a while, long enough for them to have a son together before he left, but he'd left nonetheless.

She glanced at Iva May's cottage behind her shop and the light that burned in the window.

As she walked in the back door, she made sure her outside light was on and the steps well lit, even though Iva May was only seventy. Falling and breaking something could happen quite easily, and she didn't want anything to happen to Iva May.

She'd been a wonderful neighbor and, despite their age differences, a good friend.

Anitra walked into her apartment, and Iva May stood up from the couch where the TV blasted in front of her.

Some kind of 80s sitcom with regular laugh tracks.

Anitra had watched plenty of TV with Iva May over the years, but this was a sitcom she hadn't seen too much.

She wasn't even sure the name of it.

Iva May pointed the remote at the TV, and it went blank. "Did you have a nice walk, honey?"

"I did."

She hadn't done much walking at all. She'd done much more sitting and hadn't even been staring at the water, just closed her eyes and enjoyed the closeness of human companionship.

"Your cheeks are bright red. It must be cold out." Iva May came over to the table and put a hand on the back of the chair where her purse hung.

Anitra put her hands to her cheeks. She could still feel the imprint of his fingers between hers as her hand touched the cold skin on her face.

"I guess it is. It's March. It's never that warm in Michigan in March," she said, unobtrusively taking the card out of her pocket and sticking it on top of the refrigerator.

She still didn't look at it.

She sincerely didn't want to know his name or what he did for a living. He could be a police officer, a truck driver, some kind of business dude, or an oil tycoon. She didn't care. She just appreciated a place to lay her head and forget about her burdens for a bit. That was all.

"Jordan didn't give you any trouble?" Anitra asked as Iva May picked up her purse and slung it over her shoulder.

"He never does. You put him down, and he's quiet as a church mouse." Iva May lifted her brows. "Sam brought that up. I guess they delivered it to the back door of the diner, and he'd forgotten about it." She nodded her head at the manila envelope that sat on the counter next to the microwave.

Anitra could see her lawyer's return address big and bold in the left-hand corner. She walked over, silently, and took a few minutes to read it and scan the papers while Iva May waited. Iva May had been through everything with her. She might as well go through this, too.

Anitra's bones felt like rubber as she finished looking at them and allowed her hands to drop, her head down.

Iva May slid her arm around Anitra's waist. "I didn't open it, but I don't think I need to. Those are the papers you've been waiting for, right?"

"They are. It's over." The words sounded so final she couldn't help the pang that went down through her chest and out her arms and seemed to shrink and pull her nerves all together in a jumble. A painful jumble.

It's not that she was so wrapped up in her husband anymore. She really wasn't. He hadn't been around for years.

How could she love a man who left her for someone else, then left that someone else for someone else, and on and on.

Anitra hadn't even been able to keep up with his woman-hopping until the one he was currently with got pregnant and he wanted to marry her. Hence the divorce.

But she did have feelings about a family and about having a dad for her child and having that all blow up in her face. The bills and the struggle and the work. She had feelings about that.

The papers just made everything final.

"I figured that's why you were gone a little extra long tonight."

Anitra nodded. "I suppose it was. I knew they were coming. I'm sorry. I should have told you." Her heart wavered. "I don't know how

I'm going to tell Jordan." Those last words came out on almost a sob, because she really didn't know how to tell her child. Not even that she thought he would care, but just how do you bring that up in casual conversation, "Oh, by the way, your dad is still your dad, but he's not my husband anymore."

She sighed. Most of the time, she could handle what life threw at her. What was a little harder was handling what it threw at her son.

If she could get through dealing with her son's cancer coming back, she could get through telling him she wasn't married anymore.

"Honey. I know it's hard, but you know by now it's not the end of the world," Iva May said, embracing her in a warm, spicy hug, not nearly as nice as the man's on the beach but every bit as comforting.

"I know. I just..." It was like Iva May could read her mind, but she still sighed and looked at the ceiling, not that there were any answers up there. There never had been before anyway. "I want to teach him that marriage is forever. I want to teach him that whenever you make a promise, you keep it no matter what. That it doesn't matter how hard it is to keep your promises, but when you give your word, it means something."

She was starting to develop a roll of steam, and she deliberately pulled herself back. Iva May didn't need to hear her lecture. She'd already heard it a million times.

Iva May agreed with her anyway. She'd been preaching to the choir.

"I know, honey. But you did your part. You were faithful to your husband, even after he left. You didn't go running to another man...goodness, it's been years, and you've not had anyone to help you through all the struggles you've had. Jordan can see your example and know you've done right."

She thought about the man on the beach.

Maybe she would look at the card after all.

"What if I wanted to get married again? How do I do that? How do I do that with a son who needs so much from me? There's so much I never expected I would have to handle. I'm not prepared to have a child by myself, one whose cancer could come back anytime, to run a business and juggle appointments and medications and exhaustion. I feel like such a failure as a mom."

She wasn't even making sense anymore.

"Honey, you didn't eat today, did you?"

"I didn't have time." She'd been busy baking, since weekends were their busy time when she sold most of her baked goods.

"That's one thing you can do for your son. We've talked about that before, honey. Take care of yourself. At least by eating right."

Anitra looked down. "I know. You're right. I need to do better." Thinking about everything too long made her feel overwhelmed. She needed to change the subject. "What about you? Did you ever hear from Kim? Is she coming in for Easter?" Anitra asked about Iva May's daughter.

Iva May was not fooled by her subject change but knew she needed to ease the pressure and allowed it. "I think so. She's talking about moving back." Iva May released Anitra and stepped back, her polyester pants and loose flowered blouse giving room for an expanding girth. Although Iva May was fit for seventy and didn't really need the loose clothes.

"I hope she can. Do you want me to call her?" Anitra and Kim were casual friends, with Kim being almost seven years older. Still, they couldn't come from the same small town like they did and not know each other. Especially since Iva May worked in Anitra's diner.

"I know she had a little scare, and she's telling me it's nothing, but I'm worried she's not telling me everything."

"A scare?" Anitra felt bad that she'd been so busy complaining about her divorce that she hadn't even known that anything was wrong with Kim.

"I think she had a mammogram, and they saw a shadow." Iva May's lips pursed. "At least that's what I think, reading between the lines." She shrugged. "Hopefully, I'll find out when she comes."

Fear tightened Anitra's throat, and now she was the one who stepped closer and put her arm around Iva May's shoulders that maybe were just a little softer than a younger woman's.

Over the years, with the issues with Jordan, Anitra had done a lot of research about cancer.

Not typically about women's cancers necessarily, but she knew that a woman who was diagnosed with breast cancer young often had a more aggressive form.

"Did she have a biopsy?"

"I don't know. She's telling me that it's nothing. But I'm thinking that maybe she's my only child, and she doesn't want to scare me if it's more."

"I don't think she would do that. I don't think Kim would lie. She might not tell you to protect you, but I don't think she would lie to protect you." Anitra wasn't entirely sure on this, but she felt safe enough saying it to Iva May.

Kim had always been independent but never deceitful.

Iva May nodded. "Aren't we a pair? Always borrowing trouble."

Anitra nodded, returning the small smile that Iva May gave.

She supposed, when life threw these curveballs at a person, they could respond by facing it and dealing with it or by being afraid.

So often she chose fear over action.

Whatever kind of action she could take when her divorce papers came, she wasn't sure.

"I'd better get going so you can get to bed. I'm sure you'll be up right early in the morning."

"That seems to be the way it goes. Gotta start early."

She always opened her shop early, and she often manned the counter by herself for the first hour or so as customers trickled in and she baked the day's goodies.

The upside of that was they closed at three, so she was able to spend the afternoon and evening with Jordan after he got off school.

It provided a good life for them so far. If she ended up having to pay for health insurance, that could change things.

Chapter 4

EVEN THOUGH HE DIDN'T sleep very well, John was out of bed early in the morning.

It might be vacation, he might try to take it easy, but his internal clock was set to rise at 4:30, and he couldn't usually push it back more than half an hour or so.

He'd be out making rounds in the hospital and looking at reports, or writing them, which was worse.

Not that he hated any part of his job, except losing patients. Unfortunately, because of the nature of his job, that could be a big part.

He still hadn't decided what he was going to do and hadn't spent the time he'd planned thinking about it. Since his thoughts had been on the woman at the beach.

He was old enough now, in his early forties, to know that the chances of seeing her again, especially since she wouldn't even give him her name, were almost nonexistent, and he spent a lot of the night trying to convince himself he didn't want to anyway.

He'd been given the opportunity to spearhead the start of the new oncology department at the hospital just south of Blueberry Beach.

The new trauma department, which had been made possible by a grant from a local lady, Beverly Ellis, had been extremely successful and was the premier trauma department in western Michigan.

The hospital had big plans to expand, and Blueberry Beach, while mostly known as a tourist town, was also a great place for the staff to live.

That was mostly discounting the brutal Michigan winters.

But the idyllic summers, and pleasant springs and autumns, made the winters bearable for many people.

The hospital would be a success, he was sure, and once he had the oncology department running, he would be able to scale back his hours and write the book he'd always wanted to.

Actually, he had ideas for seven or eight books. Some about patients, some about the things he learned about cancer, and some he had yet to research.

He hadn't been convinced over all the years that he'd prescribed chemo and radiation that they were actually the best way to deal with cancer.

Sometimes, they were effective, and sometimes, the cure was worse than the disease. He wanted to see cancer prevented rather than trying to cure it. That's where his mind had been going, but he couldn't just leave what he was doing without making plans for himself.

Currently, he worked in Chicago and was on the board of the oncology department there.

Not a small feat for a doctor of his age.

But he didn't like the city hospital, and he was tired of the rat race.

He needed to decide whether he wanted to take the risk of downsizing and then downsizing again.

He didn't know whether he wanted to give up what he'd worked so hard for.

And for what? More time to do what?

Write books, apparently, and he wished again that maybe he'd been a little more aggressive in his youth about dating and finding a wife and wondered if he'd let an opportunity slip by and lost it.

He laced up his running shoes, and knowing the weather here wasn't any warmer than Chicago, he wore his running tights underneath his shorts with a long-sleeved T-shirt for his jog.

Blueberry Beach had a gym. Maybe he should have gone there, but it seemed kind of silly to go to the beach and not run, even if the sunrise was on the other side of the horizon.

After a three-mile jog, where he pushed himself the last eight hundred meters, finishing strong, he still hadn't figured anything out, other than he was out of breath and ready for a coffee.

His beach house rental was three blocks down from the main street of Blueberry Beach. So he walked up the street and went into the only shop that had a light on.

The same diner he'd gone to the last two mornings that he'd been here.

The Blueberry Café. It served coffee and an eclectic mix of breakfast foods, including healthy options as well as the more traditional muffins and bagels.

They seemed to have a lot of specialty cupcakes too.

He walked in, his breathing back under control, and waited at the counter for the cashier to make her way from where she was stocking the shelves inside the glass case with what looked like fresh bagels down to the cash register and the counter where he stood.

"Good morning," she said cheerfully, her tidy gray hair looking exactly the same as it had each of the other two mornings he'd been there. "Are you having your coffee with no sugar and one cream again?" she asked, her grandmotherly smile wreathing her face in wrinkles.

"Yes please," he said. "And..."

"An egg white omelet with all the vegetables," she said, saying what he'd ordered the last two mornings.

"That's right. And a little bit of cheese."

It wasn't on the menu, but so far, they'd been happy to make it for him. It was one of the joys of small shops and another reason he knew he'd love living in Blueberry Beach.

"I'll get your coffee, and it will be just a couple minutes on that egg white omelet," the lady said.

He nodded and pulled out his wallet while she rang him up.

The cook, or baker, brought a tray of muffins out and set it on the counter against the wall.

Her hair was pulled back tight, and she wore a fitted shirt and jeans.

He'd seen her several times as he'd ordered and eaten, and he'd figured her to be younger than him. She greeted him with a smile and nod as she had the last two mornings but didn't say anything.

Maybe he was imagining it, but she seemed to turn more quickly and disappear into the kitchen with alacrity.

She seemed familiar. She hadn't when he'd first seen her, but looking at her now, he thought maybe he should recognize her.

If he moved to this community, he probably would be in here a good bit. Depending on where he eventually bought a house, maybe, but it was the only place in town open at this time in the morning, and his job required early mornings.

There was something vulnerable about the woman who disappeared, something that made him curious and kind of reminded him of the woman last night.

Although this woman looked like she had everything together, and he hardly thought that a woman who worked at a bakery would go one entire day without eating.

Maybe.

The lady behind the counter handed him his coffee. He thanked her, turning, as the bells over the door jiggled again.

He nodded his head at the crotchety-looking old man who'd come in both mornings he'd been there.

The guy had side-eyed him but hadn't said anything other than a mumbled good morning, which sounded more like a grunt than actual words.

This morning was no different.

After John sat down at his table, despite being on vacation he wished for a medical journal to peruse while he was drinking his coffee.

He pushed that idea aside and tried to focus on relaxing, which was hard. He wasn't used to doing nothing, and although he knew he needed it, it was hard to shut his brain down as it ran through all the things he needed to do.

Determined to be a people watcher, or at the very least nurse his coffee and enjoy his omelet, eating slowly, he was surprised when the old man came over and stood at his table.

"I'm Bill. Noticed you've been here the last couple mornings." The words were short. Clipped. Rough-sounding.

John nodded. That was true. When Bill didn't say anything more, he said, "I have."

Maybe Bill was waiting for a little more information, but John had no intention of giving it to him.

Some people wore their title of "doctor" like a badge of honor or maybe a badge of conceit.

He wasn't ashamed of it, but currently, he was trying to vacation. He wasn't going to walk around holding it out in front of himself so people were sure to know exactly who he was and give him the proper respect.

"Mind if I sit down?" Bill said in a grumbly voice that almost made John smile. He didn't seem like the type to want to sit down and have a friendly chitchat, but John nodded.

"Sure. Go ahead." He didn't mind the company. It would take his mind off all the things that he kept thinking he needed to do.

"I own the shop across the street," the man said, holding out his hand.

"I'm visiting," John said, taking his hand and shaking it, meeting the man's eyes, and liking that his grip was strong and firm but not aggressive.

"So you're on vacation?" Bill asked as he settled into his chair.

"I am. All week," he added, just to hold up his end of the conversation without giving anything away. "Which shop is yours?"

Bill smiled a bit. "I own the surf shop. Blueberry Surf."

John nodded and figured it was okay for him to smile a little at the name. He'd seen it, and it struck his funny bone then, too. "I haven't been in it. I guess I'll have to go check it out."

Not that he had any plans on going surfing, not now or ever, but it probably offered something beyond surfboards and whatever other equipment a surfer might need. Wetsuits maybe.

"You have to. Buy something to take home with you."

John nodded, thinking that he might know where that was going.

"And home is where?" Bill said, and John managed not to laugh. He'd seen that one coming.

"I'm in the rat race in Chicago," John finally said, which was true. Wanting to get the conversation off himself, he added, "This is a nice little town. Seems relaxed and laid-back. Did you grow up here?"

Bill shook his head. "I was born in the Upper Peninsula, pretty much raised in the woods with my folks, we had electricity but not much else. It's pretty wild up there. I liked it, but you have to do something to make a living, and my wife wasn't real fond of not having neighbors. And the winters are worse there than here, for sure."

"I say. Gotta keep the lady happy."

"Moving down here didn't keep her happy, and she left me anyway. But yeah, that's how I ended up here when I was still wet behind the ears. Had the surf shop ever since."

"Do the waves actually get high enough that you can surf on them?"

"They're not like ocean waves, and big surfers don't come here, but you can get a boogie board and have a lot of fun with it while you're here, which is what most people do. Nothing serious."

"Here's your omelet," a voice said, so familiar, so close, his head jerked up and he met the wide-open eyes of the lady who'd brought his omelet out the last two days.

It was the voice from last night. He was sure of it.

But...was this her?

She didn't seem to recognize him, and in the dark, he hadn't seen her well enough to be able to tell. Not to mention her hair was pulled back, and now she had a ball cap pulled very low over her face.

In fact, as soon as their eyes met, she moved her head, and the brim of her cap blocked his view of her face.

"Is there anything else I can get you?" she asked as she set a bottle of ketchup down in front of him.

He couldn't think of a thing. He wanted to say something to get her to move her face, but nothing was coming to mind, and she turned her attention to his companion.

"Good morning, Bill. Looks like it's going to be a busy day. The sunrise was pretty."

"It's going to be a terrible day," Bill said. "There was no sunrise. The clouds blocked it."

The lady last night had been whispering and talking low. This lady seemed cheerful, and her voice, while similar to last night, was bright and held humor.

"I think you must be talking about yesterday morning. This morning was clear."

He couldn't see her eyes, but she shifted her head, and he could see a little smile hovering around her mouth.

Bill's words were gruff, but there was a trace of humor in his voice, too.

John got the feeling that this might be a conversation that they had quite often. And it seemed to be one they both enjoyed.

"I'm going to pack up everything and move to Florida. No point staying here. Weather's terrible, and the tourists are rude."

"I'm sure Randall will be moved into your shop before you're completely moved out. But I'll miss you." The lady smiled. "Good to see you, Bill."

She turned and walked away.

"Good to see you too, kid," Bill said gruffly to her back.

She raised her hand but didn't turn.

The whole exchange had made John curious, but before he could say anything, long pink nails clicked down on the table beside him, and a voice, somewhat sultry, said, "Is this seat taken?"

"It sure is. Can't you see that's my twin brother sitting there?" The bit of humor that had been in Bill's voice when he had been bantering with the cook was gone.

"Your twin brother died fifty years ago," the voice said, and then the fingers lifted off the table, and a hand stretched in front of John's face, rings on four of the five fingers and several bracelets gracing the slender wrist.

Somehow, as he studied her hand, it seemed almost helpless.

He wondered if it was by design.

And then he couldn't figure out how someone could make their hand deliberately look helpless.

"My name is Chanel, and I am at your service," Chanel said as her hand waved gently in front of his face.

He took the fingers that were offered and half wondered if he was supposed to kiss them. That kind of seemed like what she might be expecting, but he turned his hand sideways and clasped hers in a handshake. "John," he said simply.

"Isn't it a beautiful morning, boys," she said as she sat down carefully, the way John imagined a princess might settle into her throne as she perched in front of her adoring subjects.

John shot a glance at Bill, who looked perturbed and not appreciative of their guest.

So John answered. "It's a beautiful morning. I enjoyed a run on the beach. I take it you must be a shop owner?"

"Oh, I dabble in the Blueberry Clothing Store down the street, but I really don't have to work. I only do so because I enjoy it," Chanel said, her words ringing in such a way that John wondered whether they were actually true.

She lifted her hand and gracefully brushed a stray hair back away from her face. Her hair was piled on her head in such a way that it seemed to be deliberately falling loose, but John didn't know much about women's hairstyles and couldn't say for sure.

He'd been looking forward to talking to Bill, and asking Bill about the cook, and trying to find out if she might have been the person he saw last night on the beach.

But Chanel launched into a story about two kids fighting over a banana in her shop, and as they pulled the banana apart, it flew up in the air and came down, landing in her cleavage.

Bill had gotten up during her story and given a wave goodbye, like he'd heard the story before and wasn't going to sit around and listen to the rest of it.

John laughed at the right time, and the idea actually was kind of funny, but he thought maybe the story was designed to get him to look at her cleavage, and it just made him eat his omelet faster than he had intended to.

Regardless, he left the diner thinking his original idea was probably accurate: forget about the girl on the beach.

Chapter 5

ANITRA BLINKED AT HER computer screen. She blinked again, like blinking would make the numbers that she was seeing disappear and the correct numbers reappear.

She checked her account again. It was the checking account she always used. She reconciled it every month.

It wasn't her business account but her personal account, where she kept her paychecks and had been building up a solid nest egg.

It was linked to the savings account that she and her ex shared, but as far as she knew, he hadn't been using it.

Except that wasn't true anymore.

Because, in the last fifteen seconds, she realized he *had* been using it.

Just once. He'd used it once, and he drained it, all but ten dollars.

Horror, in the seconds since she'd seen it and figured out what happened, had been replaced in her chest by anger.

But underneath the anger was a fear, fear of the unknown, fear of what was going to happen now, fear that she might not get it back.

She could go to her lawyer, and Danny would be forced to return it.

He'd essentially stolen it from her, except it had been taken out a week ago before their divorce had been finalized.

She didn't know all the ins and outs, and she wouldn't until she saw her lawyer, but in her experience, it was going to cost her probably half of what he'd taken just to get it back.

She put her head down on the desk. How much more was she going to have to take?

The man couldn't just step quietly out of her life. Oh no, he had to take her money with him.

Man, she'd been stupid. Never fall in love with a tourist. Never never never.

That wasn't fair. There were plenty of nice people who came through. Hundreds every summer, even thousands.

They were nice, and she loved talking to them, and learning about where they came from, and hearing about how they loved Blueberry Beach, and just having a really great time. Learning about people and getting to know them. And yes, she had friends that she saw every year, and she loved them.

It wasn't fair to hate all tourists just because her husband had been a jerk. Because she had other bad experiences.

Not many.

Most of them had been good. Why couldn't she focus on the good?

That didn't even matter now. Her propensity to think about things that didn't matter when she had life-and-death issues to deal with was annoying.

What was she going to do without that money?

At least her bills were all paid for this month. She hadn't really needed the money—it was her cushion. That was what she was going to rely on if she had to pay health insurance and if it was more than what she was anticipating. And if any other little unexpected expenses came up.

Her head was going in circles, and her stomach had a sick, bottomless feeling that she hated.

She closed her computer, but she hadn't gotten up from her chair when Iva May walked in.

"I'm sorry, honey. Did you send me a message and I missed it?" she asked when she saw Anitra was sitting at her desk and not dressed to walk.

"No. I'm sorry. I do want to go for a walk. I just got distracted by some work I was trying to get done. Accounting." She stood with a little smile on her face. Iva May knew exactly how much she hated accounting. It was her least favorite part of being a business owner.

"Goodness. I guess it is the end of the month. Time to start thinking about next month's bills, I guess. Thanks for reminding me," she said in a little bit of an ironic tone that said she didn't want to be reminded.

They chatted a bit more, with Anitra explaining that Jordan had a headache and had gone to bed early. It broke her heart to see him in pain and so exhausted, and she'd spent an extra minute or two lingering by his bedside, watching as he slept.

With that, and this latest and last blow from Danny, Anitra couldn't wait to get out, to stand in front of the vastness of Lake Michigan and feel like herself and her problems weren't nearly as big as they felt to her.

Maybe she wanted to be distracted again, as she'd been earlier in the week, with the kind and compassionate man who'd sat beside her and held her like she meant something.

She thought the man that she'd seen yesterday in the diner had been the man she'd seen on the beach.

He wasn't good-looking in a drop-dead gorgeous kind of way, but he looked solid, and wholesome, and honest. An upright man. A man who had integrity.

When she'd given him his omelet, she'd almost asked if he'd been on the beach, but she hadn't wanted to. Or maybe hadn't gotten her nerve up.

But when she'd brought out the tray of scones, she had made up her mind that she was going to go over and introduce herself. Except, he'd been sitting with Chanel, and they'd been laughing.

It changed her mind immediately, and she hadn't come back out of the kitchen until he left.

She had made sure she hadn't seen him again, although he'd been in her shop.

Now, with her money issues and Jordan's cancer, that man was the least of her worries.

At least he should be.

She wasn't completely broke, because she had the deposit for today and a little bit stashed away, just because it had become habit while she was married to have a secret stash since her husband had a tendency to spend money without talking to her.

It was something they fought about.

She tried to put it in perspective. It wasn't as bad as having her son diagnosed with cancer.

But she needed to be able to take care of her family.

Running into her small bedroom, she changed her clothes, trying to shed her worries with her jeans, letting her hair down, and slipping on sandals.

"Thank you," she said to Iva May as she waved at her and walked out the door.

She wore the same tunic that she typically did when she walked on the beach.

She loved the way it blew in the breeze and almost made it so she could *see* the wind and not just feel it.

The wind felt great through her hair, almost massaging her scalp, since she had to keep it up while working.

She tried to focus on the little things, the wind that grew stronger as she crested the dunes and came out on the beach, the soft feel of the sand under her feet when she kicked her sandals off, picking them up and holding them with two fingers, the moon on the water. It was slightly more full, maybe not three quarters, and each ripple of the water reflected it back.

The sky was clear, the stars bright.

Enjoying life meant letting go of the things that felt huge and wrong and enjoying the smaller things, like moonlight on water, and sand under her toes, and wind that billowed her dress and blew her hair and moved across her cheeks with such a soft caress that she closed her eyes.

The smell of fresh lake water, and another day with satisfied customers, and good food.

It didn't negate her husband's treachery, and the anger still simmered in her heart and the back of her throat, boiling just under the surface in her chest. But she couldn't spend the rest of her life angry at her spouse, ex-spouse, and she couldn't let him ruin today, like he'd ruined so many yesterdays.

She'd missed the sunset, since Jordan had stayed at a friend's after school and she'd needed to pick him up, and now there was just an orange glow on the very far horizon.

Still, the three-quarters moon kept the beach glowing, and she had no trouble seeing as she walked out.

It was a little chillier than it had been earlier in the week, and the beach was deserted.

Having just come through the Michigan winter, Anitra almost felt warm; she wasn't cold.

Even the brisk breeze that hardly ever stopped did not chill her.

She walked out to the firm sand right at the edge of the water and turned, starting toward the pier.

It wasn't far away, which was a good thing since she really didn't feel like walking. She felt like curling up in a ball and pretending that something good was happening.

It would take a lot of imagination, but she tried to put a positive spin on it and to resolve that this was the last time that her husband was going to take anything from her.

Her ex-husband.

Breathing deeply of lake air, she walked along against the wind, her skirt blowing around her legs.

Sometimes, she walked up on the pier, sitting on the edge with her legs dangling, but tonight, she stopped just a little ways away and stood facing the lake, just thinking about how it would be here long after her problems were solved. Long after she was gone.

Thinking about how the problems that she had really weren't that big, even though they seemed that way to her.

And how, somehow, they would work out. And she would be stronger and better because of them.

She believed it. With her whole heart, she believed it, it just didn't make going through them any easier.

"I kinda hoped I'd see you here tonight."

Anitra turned at the voice, already knowing who it was and feeling her lips curve up while her heart straightened.

"You weren't here last night," she said, then thought she gave away too much with that statement. She'd been looking for him.

"It was raining."

"I see. You're a fair-weather beach walker." She allowed the tease in her voice, trying to sink into the ease of the conversation, just wanting to enjoy it and stop worrying about things she had no control over.

"Wow. If you were out here last night, you're hard-core."

"The lake is beautiful when it's boiling and tossing. There's a lot to see. It's fun to sit on the pier and watch it."

"You would freeze to death."

She laughed. It hadn't been below freezing. "I suppose hypothermia could be an issue if you stay too long."

"You never do?"

"Not usually."

He stopped in front of her and then turned and stood shoulder to shoulder with her as they looked out at the water together.

She hadn't forgotten him sitting at the table laughing with Chanel, but why not?

Why couldn't he? He could talk to her, he could talk to Chanel, he could talk to anyone he wanted. There was no reason why not.

Maybe she'd been a little disappointed, because Chanel was a flirt. She wanted her mystery man to see through that.

She should have known better. Men never could. Women didn't seem to have a problem, like they had a beacon that alerted them to flirts and women who were dishonest or something, but there weren't too many men that could read someone like Chanel and know exactly what she wanted.

Or maybe he was just too polite to get up when she sat down with him.

Regardless, that was the very least, the absolute least of Anitra's worries, and other than not going back out to his table until he was gone, she hadn't let it bother her.

Although, she kept it in mind tonight.

She didn't want another man who was happy with anyone and the more the merrier.

She'd been there and she'd done that, and she was absolutely not interested in doing it again.

But if that were the kind of man he was, he wasn't interested in permanence. Just a fling, no matter how much her instinct was telling her different.

"You're quiet tonight."

"It's pretty. Maybe I'm just enjoying it."

"Glad you're doing that on your feet and not facedown in the sand."

"I guess a girl will never live that down, will she?" Anitra asked, allowing a little smile in her voice, liking how talking to him made her problems that seemed so large go away.

There was nothing wrong with chatting and enjoying it.

"I guess not when I won't let her." He looked over, the moonlight shining on the angles of his face. "I'm sorry. I didn't mean to rub anything in."

"You weren't. I was just poking fun at myself. And you a little as well."

"I suspected, but I didn't want to assume. Sometimes, people can't laugh at themselves."

"Goodness. If I can't laugh at myself, I wouldn't have much to laugh at."

"That bad?"

"No. It's not. I won't let it be," she said, meaning it. Maybe the words came a little more forcefully and with less humor than she intended.

"All right. Remind me not to get in your way."

"I don't think I'm that fearsome. I just...I'm just not gonna let life win, you know?"

"I guess."

She turned to face him, the wind whipping her hair into her face and her skirt billowing around his legs. "I want to thank you for the other night. I don't usually get to sit beside someone, and put my head on their shoulder, and feel safe and protected. It was a nice little bit of time, and I've had a sweet memory."

His throat bobbed as he swallowed and took another step closer to her. His foot brushed against hers, and she realized he was in his bare feet.

His hand came up, pushing her hair out of her face, then sliding down and staying on her neck, warm against the chilly air.

"I guess I feel like I'm the one that should be thanking you. It's a sweet memory for me too."

"I don't normally do that."

"I know. I think you might have mentioned that at the time." His thumb stroked over the edge of her jaw. "I'm not sure if I said that I don't normally do that, either, but it's true. Did you ever look at my card?"

She shook her head. She hadn't. As far as she knew, it was still on top of the refrigerator where she put it. "I didn't want to ruin anything."

"How?"

"By making it real. I just want it to be a dream. The problems are gone, it's just an innocent time of companionship."

"Tonight's my last night here."

She nodded, trying to push aside the disappointment that wanted to clutch at her chest. "People come and go. Happens all the time."

"I...I didn't want to be just like everyone else."

Her eyes searched his, but the moon was behind him, and his face was in shadow. Maybe his words were a little unsure, and while she wanted to reassure him, she'd seen it too often, and she couldn't.

"You go back home, and this will just be a happy memory of your vacation. Nothing more."

"If that's all you let it be."

Maybe he was sincere. People often were. They said they'd stay in touch. They never did. But life had been weighing her down, and she wanted to believe...she didn't even know what she wanted to believe. She didn't have time for romance, not long-distance with someone who lived...she didn't even know where. He could be from Montana, or Iowa, or Texas.

Somewhere far away, and she might never see him again.

Maybe it was the night. Maybe it was the divorce papers that were still sitting on her counter. Maybe it was the drained bank account and the knowledge that she had no idea what she was going to do. Maybe it was anxiety over the test results that had come back positive, confirming that her child's chances of having a normal life were slim to none, or maybe it was just the man.

Knowing she shouldn't, she stepped closer and put a hand on his chest.

"You really think you're coming back?" she asked.

His eyes darkened, but they narrowed too, like he wasn't sure what she was doing and wasn't sure he would like it. "I know I will. You can count on it."

"Next year this time." It wasn't a question.

"No. Sooner than that. Two months, three at most. I'll be back."

His other arm came around her, and she wanted to lay her head on his chest like before, but she didn't. Because everything in her life felt off-kilter and wrong, and although she knew she was making one more huge mistake on top of all the other mistakes she'd made, she wanted to believe that just for tonight, all of her problems could go away, just for a little bit, in the arms of a good man.

Faulty thinking, her brain screamed, but his arms were warm and strong, and maybe he wasn't as honorable as he looked, but she wanted reality to go away.

"I don't want to know your name," she said.

"I want to know yours," he answered.

"Will you do something for me?" she asked.

He hesitated before he answered, as though weighing his words and not wanting to promise more than he could give.

She hoped that's what it was. She liked that. She didn't want words. She wanted action. She was tired of words that didn't mean anything. Tired of people who didn't keep their word. Tired of being lied to. Tired of being stolen from.

Tired.

"Anything. If I can. Anything for you."

She wanted to ask for something hard then, just to see if he'd actually do it. But she didn't want to be disappointed.

"Kiss me."

Maybe there was surprise in his eyes, she couldn't say for sure, but as he lowered his head, he said, "I thought you would ask me for something hard."

She didn't tell him that wasn't all she wanted, wasn't all she intended, and she was pretty sure he didn't know as his head lowered toward hers, and their lips touched.

Chapter 6

MONDAY MORNING, JOHN had an iPad and had just walked out of the patient's room, after having done one of the things he absolutely hated.

Delivering the news that a person's child had cancer and outlining the treatment options. Those appointments always took a long time, and they took a lot of tissues.

They matched his mood, though, although he didn't find it hard to be compassionate.

Sometimes, life didn't work out the way he thought it should.

Not that he'd ever been diagnosed with a disease that could kill him. He should be grateful.

With the job that he had, usually gratefulness for his life and blessings wasn't hard.

He set his iPad down on the big counter, and the receptionist looked up.

"Your 10:30 appointment canceled. I've rescheduled him for tomorrow, and your 11 o'clock isn't here yet."

"Thanks. I'm taking a walk."

Normally, he might have chatted a little more with Bonnie. She was a nice lady and had been the receptionist as long as he'd been here. She knew her job, and she was good at it.

Patients enjoyed her. She was compassionate and able to step in at times. Normally, she could coax a smile out of most children as well.

He went to the elevator without taking his white lab coat off and pushed the button for the eleventh floor.

Typically, he'd found the eleventh floor was not very busy, and there was a beautiful waiting room, with lots of plants and big windows overlooking the city of Chicago and facing the western side of Lake Michigan.

More than once, when he needed a break, that's where he'd gone.

There were, scattered throughout the hospital, plenty of break rooms for doctors to get away.

In his specialty, it was almost a necessity. But this waiting room on the eleventh floor was right beside the chapel, and he knew he needed to spend some time on his knees.

The morning had been terrible.

The elevator doors opened, and he'd intended to go and stand by the window, looking out over the city of Chicago. Seeing Lake Michigan from the other side.

Normally, he watched the sunrise over it rather than see it set, but he didn't go to the windows.

He went straight to the chapel that adjoined the waiting room. It was deserted as it usually was, and he walked down the middle aisle, past the five rows of pews, and went to his knees on the first row.

It was one of those times where he couldn't pray. Couldn't think. Didn't have words.

The Holy Spirit was supposed to make groanings that couldn't be uttered, and this had to be one of those times.

What had he done?

All his life, he'd been so careful.

Sure, he wanted God to send someone for him, wanted her to be there, but not like that. Not like he'd done on Saturday night.

All he could say was, "I'm sorry."

Apologizing to the Lord, but he needed to apologize to the lady, only he didn't know her name.

The kiss they'd shared had turned into more, and he hadn't meant for it to.

He didn't know what she'd meant to happen.

He wasn't sure how he felt about her either.

Except, she'd been someone he couldn't stop thinking about.

She had the sadness on her face that he saw in mothers' faces every day.

He didn't know if it was a child with cancer or some other problem, but he did know she was facing it alone.

By choice, since he had been willing to talk to her about it, whatever it was.

She'd shut him out on that end.

And then done something, *they'd* done something, that he never intended.

Words weren't enough. Words were inadequate.

The wood flooring dug into his knees as the pew's hard wood dug into his elbows. He put his hands together and set his forehead on his folded hands.

He didn't know what to do. Didn't know how to reach her. And hadn't been fast enough to stop her when she left.

It had been a simple matter for her to throw her dress over her head and run from him.

Her request that he not follow her had stopped him long enough to give her the head start she needed, and then his struggle with his own clothes had given her the rest of the time to disappear.

Possibly forever.

"I thought I'd find you in here, John," a voice said, and John closed his eyes before he opened them and raised his head.

"Stephen. You need me?"

He didn't get off the floor. Didn't rise from his humble position. Wasn't nearly done. Hadn't even managed to get a coherent sentence out to the Lord.

"Not really. I just noticed that you seem a little distracted today, and when you left, I figured I would see if there was something I could do."

Stephen had been like a mentor to him. Ten years older, with more experience, he'd been the one that John had talked to about the opportunity that he had in Blueberry Beach.

He'd already emailed the board and let them know that he'd made the decision to transfer.

It should be a six-month stint, and then he would transition to less hours.

Maybe he was making a wrong decision, but he'd finally gotten his medical school loans all paid off, and in all that time, there still wasn't anything that would hold him in Chicago.

Other than his work here, and his patients whom he loved.

"I saw you made your decision." Stephen sat down beside where John knelt by the pew.

"Yeah. It was a tough one."

"I know you agonized over it. But I think you're making the right one."

"Yeah. I think I need to slow down some and live life, or it's going to end up passing me by..."

He hadn't quite intended to live life the way he had Saturday night.

He wasn't naïve. Lots of people lived that way. Through college and even medical school, he'd seen it over and over. No one gave it a second thought.

And that was fine for them. It was their lives and their choices.

He'd lived a different kind of life and had made a different choice. And he'd stuck to it. Until Saturday night.

"I can't say that you're making a wrong decision. If I were younger, I might be thinking about getting out too. But my life's work is here, and I want to keep going."

"I understand that. I'll miss you."

Stephen crossed his legs and put an arm on the back of the pew as he leaned back. "I thought you might be having second thoughts. You seemed distracted today."

"No. It has nothing to do with that."

Actually, it might have had a little bit to do with it. The email that he'd composed Sunday morning and sent to the board so they had it in their inboxes first thing on Monday had been a result of a decision that he'd made as a result of what he'd done Saturday night.

It was the decision he had been leaning toward anyway, but that settled it.

Maybe there was no future for him with her, whatever her name was, but regardless, he wasn't changing his mind and he wasn't giving up the opportunity to move closer to her. Plus, that was what he had wanted to do anyway.

"Is it something you want to talk about?" Stephen asked, his voice compassionate, and John knew he would listen.

"No. Sometimes, we do things, and we realize after we do them that they are one of those mistakes that will haunt you for the rest of your life, you know?"

"Yeah. I know. I've made some of those myself." Stephen uncrossed his legs and leaned forward. "Did you make a wrong diagnosis? Did you miss a shadow?"

"No. Nothing like that." He had. Everyone had. He could say the exact number of times he had, because it was something that one didn't forget. Sometimes, missing a shadow on an original x-ray meant the difference between life and death.

He always tried to be very thorough in his diagnoses.

"Well, all right. I'm here if you need me."

"I know. And you know I'll come to you if you need me to."

"I know. I guess the wheels are set in motion. Another month, two at the most, and you will be on the other side of the lake," Stephen said, slapping his legs and standing up.

John nodded. Two months would go by quickly, but right now, they felt like forever.

It didn't matter though; there was nothing he could do to make Saturday night disappear. He couldn't do anything to make it right either.

Stephen walked out. And John bowed his head again, still unsure of what to say.

Part of the problem was, as much as he knew it was wrong, as much as he regretted it, as much as he wished he could make it right, he couldn't say he wished it didn't happen. Because that would be a lie.

Chapter 7

TWO MONTHS LATER

Anitra walked beside Jordan, carefully following the instructions she'd been given at the information desk.

Typically, when he had an appointment, they'd gone to Chicago, where they'd gone for all of his treatments.

With the new oncology department opening up in the Blueberry Beach Hospital, she'd agreed to be transferred here, under the instructions of Dr. John Chambers. She had been assured that he was a top-notch physician and one of the best pediatric oncologists that Chicago had had on staff.

He'd left his job in Chicago expressly to open up the oncology department in Blueberry Beach Hospital and oversee it, implementing all procedures followed in Chicago.

Jordan was one of the first children to be a patient in the pediatric wing, and Dr. Chambers would be heading up the team that would oversee his care.

They had been very clear with her. Some of the doctors who would be treating Jordan would be in training.

During her phone consultation, they'd also been very clear with her. His cancer was growing, quickly, and would not respond to chemo.

At this appointment, she had been told to expect that she would have to choose hospice or she would be given some options for experimental treatments.

Iva May was managing the diner today, and Anitra's mom walked on the other side of Jordan.

Once the doctors had done a perfunctory checkup on Jordan, her mom would take him out, and she would face the doctor alone.

Jordan knew his cancer was back. But she hadn't told him anything else. Even so, despite his advanced age of nine years, his hand had slipped into hers and gripped it tightly.

Several years ago, he'd announced he was too old to hold her hand, but the importance of today, no matter what she'd not told him, had not been lost on him, and even a boy of nine needed his mother when cancer slipped its insidious tentacles throughout the reaches of his young body.

Still, yesterday, he'd wanted to sign up for summer baseball, and she hadn't been able to tell him no.

She hoped at this appointment they could tell her about an experimental treatment that would work, because she didn't want to give up hope.

She was afraid she was going to be given a lifespan estimate instead.

How did a parent deal with being told her young child's life was going to end before it had really even begun?

Swallowing hard, she lifted her chin and glanced down at her little boy when he tugged on her hand.

"This hospital smells funny."

She put on a smile, the kind of smile that felt fake and forced like she was smiling through plastic wrap but hopefully looked real to him. "All hospitals smell funny, don't they?"

"It smells different than my hospital."

She never dreamed that her son would have a hospital that he called "mine."

She nodded. "You're right. It does."

"I think all hospitals have their own funny smell," her mom said.

Their eyes met over the top of Jordan's head. Her mom knew exactly what could potentially be happening as well as she.

They hadn't talked about it though.

She wouldn't have been able to keep her business going without Iva May and her mother helping her.

Typically a hairdresser, her mom had alternately watched Jordan, baked, and worked the counter along with Iva May. She'd picked up whatever slack she needed to and had worked tirelessly for Anitra while still trying to keep her own beauty shop open.

Anitra appreciated every second her mom had spared for her.

"Oh, look!" Jordan said, pointing to a big mural of a beach and a lake. Anitra noted the blueberry bushes that were painted in rows on the far left of the mural.

She had to smile at that.

They were everywhere around Blueberry Beach.

The climate wasn't exactly hospitable, but the ground was perfect for raising blueberries—slightly acidic and sandy as well. With the lake nearby, the water table was high, with plenty of availability to irrigate.

Blueberries were good for people, with lots of antioxidants and other healthy things. No matter how many they'd eaten, they hadn't been enough to keep her son from getting cancer.

They turned at the arrow, went through heavy double doors with thick glass panes, and walked up to the reception desk. She checked Jordan in while he and her mother went to the waiting area.

The toys were new and interesting, although he had outgrown many of them. Anitra was glad there didn't seem to be a long wait.

She hated hospitals. Hated being in them. Hated the memories they contained. Mostly bad.

She put her hand over her stomach and willed it to stop rolling.

She'd figured out almost two weeks after that Saturday night on the beach that she couldn't make a mistake like that without it having consequences.

What a way to celebrate her divorce.

They hadn't been sitting there long when the nurse called them back.

She was older with a friendly smile. Anitra liked her immediately, but everything just felt different, and with as nervous as she already was about the appointment, she almost longed for the drive to Chicago and the familiar hospital there.

The nurse turned, giving Jordan a smile and chatting about school, asking how it was going and if he was done for the year.

He told her how he was out of school and was hoping to play baseball this summer, and his mom was going to sign him up for the team as soon as the doctor said it was okay.

It was times like this that made Anitra want to cry.

She swallowed hard and breathed in slowly through her nose.

She could get through this.

She felt a touch on her arm and looked over at her mom giving her a concerned look.

She pulled up another one of those plastic-wrap smiles and gave a little shake of her head to indicate that she was going to be fine.

She was. Going to be fine that was. Eventually.

Although she would never be the same.

Part of her heart was slowly being cut out of her chest.

She couldn't think about that either. So many things she couldn't think about.

The nurse indicated the door they were to enter, and the three of them went in. Jordan knew he was to go on the table, and he hopped up, not as spry as he had been in months past. Anitra could see it and wished she couldn't. Just one more piece of evidence that shouted that they needed to be here.

Anitra handed him the Gatorade bottle she carried all the time, constantly trying to get him to drink something to keep him hydrated.

He was skinny, with his head too big for his body, but he was still a boy. He moved around on the paper to make it crinkle and waved away the Gatorade she offered.

The nurse did all the normal things, asking questions and typing in answers, and eventually she stood up, gave Jordan one last smile, and said, "The doctor will be right in."

She looked specifically at Anitra. "I have a note here that says someone explained to you that there will be a team of doctors coming in, and Dr. Chambers—our best—will be coordinating. He's from Chicago, and he's very good."

The nurse gave her a reassuring smile as she nodded her head. Then, after Anitra's nod, she left, closing the door behind her.

When Jordan had been younger, waiting in the doctor's office had been somewhat difficult, if it lasted too long, since his attention span was short, and he hated being cooped up.

Now that he was a little older, he was better able to sit still. Plus, after so much time spent in hospitals and doctors' offices, he knew the drill.

Or maybe he just didn't have the energy he used to.

He sat kind of slumped on the table, and Anitra watched with worry as his eyes drifted closed.

He had been sleeping a lot, taking naps during the day.

That wasn't uncommon when he was having treatments, but it still wasn't normal, and it worried her.

There was murmuring and voices outside the door for a few minutes before there was a knock, and it opened.

Anitra recognized the man who strode in first immediately.

She kept her gasp from escaping by sheer will and put her hand over her stomach, very afraid for a few long moments that she was going to be sick.

Thankfully, her mother didn't notice, because her eyes were on the doctors as they walked in.

There were four of them, including Dr. Chambers, who most definitely was the man at the beach.

Maybe she wouldn't have recognized him, if she hadn't seen him in the diner too. At the beach, his face had been in shadow. Even with everything that came later—she would never forget his gentleness, his consideration, the way his body moved with hers, and the way his touch and his voice made her feel cherished and adored.

She shoved back against the memories, wanting more than ever to cry.

Her inclination was to duck her head, but she blinked and lifted her chin instead.

Maybe he wouldn't notice her with her new haircut and with his doctor persona on.

Maybe he would and wouldn't care.

She would prefer the first and couldn't believe the second.

When she'd gotten up to run away, he'd begged her to stay.

Her lungs couldn't seem to fill, and her instinct begged her to run again.

But they were here to talk about Jordan, and she had to push all of that aside, along with the guilt that pinched at the back of her throat, as she forced her hand away from her stomach.

Dr. Chambers had greeted Jordan right away and then looked at her mother and her, offering his hand.

She thought she saw a flicker as their eyes met, but his doctor façade did not crumble, and if he recognized her, she couldn't tell.

"I'm Dr. Chambers, and you must be Jordan's mother."

"I am. And this is my mother, Glenna."

Each of the other doctors introduced themselves, and Dr. Chambers said, "This feels like a big team, I'm sure. You're not used to having this many people involved, but we're opening a new oncology department, which obviously you've heard about, and I'm responsible for training the new doctors in the procedures that we use at our award-winning pediatric oncology department in Chicago."

His voice was businesslike, although it held tones of compassion. Anitra nodded her head and listened intently, focusing on his words and how they would affect her child.

Dr. Chambers was excellent with Jordan, and while Jordan had very good reasons to hate hospitals and doctors, he didn't. Dr. Chambers had him laughing in the five or ten minutes he spent with them.

Then, he stepped back and said, "All right, Jordan, you can hop down and go with your grandmother while I have a little chat with your mom."

"Don't forget, tell her that I can play baseball," Jordan said, in a very businesslike tone, before he jumped down and wobbled some. Anitra rose half out of her chair to catch him before he caught his balance, flashed her a grin, and opened the door, walking out with the confidence of a childhood that had spent many days in a hospital and doctors' offices.

A little smile hovered around Dr. Chambers's lips as Jordan skipped out.

"Good kid," he said as he turned back to her.

Something that seemed like a shadow flickered in his eyes. Was it recognition?

If she had looked at the card that was still facedown on top of her refrigerator, she wouldn't have been caught flat-footed like she had been.

It didn't exactly surprise her that he might not recognize her. She supposed if she had any feminine vanity at all, she might be a little offended.

But all she wanted right now was to take care of Jordan. For him to get better.

Maybe it was her imagination that Dr. Chambers stared at her a little longer than necessary before he cleared his throat and looked down at his iPad.

She shoved the baggage that she carried, embarrassment at her stupidity and weakness, among other things, aside and listened with a sinking heart as he talked about Jordan and showed her the two scans showing the cancer had grown at an alarmingly fast rate.

He mentioned there were several studies that Jordan could possibly be eligible for, but none of them were producing great results. They were making the children who were enrolled in them more miserable. Their quality of life was terrible, and he said that he would not recommend them.

Anitra swallowed. This is where she wished she had someone beside her to hold her hand and to support her. A shoulder to lean on. Arms to hold her. Someone to share the burden and sorrow and decisions with.

But it was just her, so she lifted her head, looked him in the eye, and said, "How long does he have?"

Dr. Chambers didn't seem surprised by her question. She supposed he was probably expecting it.

"Maybe a month. Possibly up to three." His eyes didn't waver. "I recommend getting hospice in immediately."

His tone held compassion, and she recognized that even as the room spun around her.

But she'd fallen in front of him once, and that's what had started this whole terrible side road toward a place she hadn't wanted to go.

Of course, what was done was done, and she couldn't undo it. It wasn't his fault. It most definitely wasn't his fault.

It was all her.

A thought went through her mind, just a question... Would Jordan's cancer have come back if she hadn't—in that moment of weakness—made that decision?

Dr. Chambers spoke some more. About hospice and things he recommended, and went through typical recommendations until hospice could get set up regarding the pain that Jordan had at night in particular.

Somehow, she managed to listen and even asked several questions, although she knew she'd be getting a full printout of everything he'd said.

Indeed, after he was done speaking with her, he sat at the computer and typed, speaking occasionally to the doctors behind him but mostly typing and asking an occasional question.

When he was done, he looked again at her and asked, "Do you have any other questions or concerns?"

She thought long and hard. She had lots of concerns and a few questions, but none that he could answer.

She shook her head.

He nodded. Then he looked at the group of doctors behind him. "You can go ahead and go. I want to have a private word with Mrs. Pollard."

Anitra wasn't so upset that she didn't see the surprise that lifted the faces of the doctors standing there, but they obediently turned and filed out.

When the door shut behind them, Dr. Chambers turned to her.

She thought for sure he had recognized her, and now there would be a reckoning.

It was the last thing she wanted. She had absolutely zero desire to talk about that night, or the consequences, or a relationship, or anything.

All she wanted was to get her son and hold him and somehow make it so that the cancer went into her body instead of his.

Except, she had another life to protect; she couldn't take his cancer even if such a thing were possible.

"Mrs. Pollard, I know these last days are going to be hard."

She tried not to cringe when he said "last days."

"Your family has already been through a lot with Jordan's treatments and everything that he's been through. It's been a long road." He indicated the computer that held Jordan's records. Dr. Chambers was the best, and Anitra was sure he knew all of Jordan's history. "If it's possible at all, try to relax and take it easy as a family."

If her husband hadn't stolen her money, if her lawyer had been successful in getting it back, if she didn't have a business to run, if she weren't carrying another child...maybe she would have done that.

But it was impossible.

"Sometimes, parents end up almost as sick as their children from the worry and stress. I just want to warn you and encourage you to talk to our counselors and make use of everything that's available. There are a lot of great programs. Things are just starting here, so they're eager to have people joining. You'll be well taken care of."

She nodded, not meeting his eyes, clenching her teeth together because she was not going to cry. Not in this office. Not in front of this man.

Unfortunately, her hormones were fighting her tooth and nail. So far, she was winning.

He stood and held out his hand. "If there's anything I can do, please get in touch." His tone was more businesslike. As their hands shook, he tilted his head. "Do I know you from somewhere? Did I meet you in Chicago?"

"No," she said honestly. "We never met in Chicago."

He nodded, like that was what he was expecting to hear.

"You just seem familiar. I'm sorry I don't have better news," he said as he reached for the doorknob.

She was too.

Chapter 8

JOHN WALKED UP THE street, his breathing becoming more normal. Three miles was typical for him, although it was slightly more work to run on the beach than it was on a treadmill or along the road, which is what he had normally done before he moved.

The new oncology wing at the hospital in Blueberry Beach had a very nice exercise room, and he'd made use of it, usually late at night.

Moving from Chicago and setting up the new department had been extremely time-consuming and very involved.

He had been sure he'd get back to Blueberry Beach before this.

It had been over two months since the night he'd left.

The woman had accused him of never coming back. He had been determined at the time to prove her wrong. He'd returned, but he hadn't expected it to be this long.

Just a few more months, if things continued to go as smoothly as they were now, and he would be able to back off a little from his commitments at the hospital and start taking time to write his book.

He could picture himself sitting at the diner drinking coffee and writing, waiting for the mystery woman to walk in.

She had to be local. Had to be.

His steps slowed as he got closer to the café. The neon sign that was typically lit in the window was dark.

All the windows were dark.

He got close enough to read the "closed" sign on the door.

Odd.

Of course, he didn't know much about lakeside towns, but he would have assumed that the closer they got to summer, the busier it would be.

Strange that it would be closed so late on a beautiful May morning.

He looked at his watch and noted the time was almost seven.

He was even later today than he had been the other times he'd come earlier in the spring.

"She's closed indefinitely because of some family issues," a voice said beside him, and he turned, seeing the somewhat grumpy older man who'd sat down beside him in the diner the last time he was there finish walking across the street. "I'm Bill, by the way."

"I'm John. I remember you from earlier this spring." John shook Bill's hand. "Indefinitely?" he asked, thinking about the lady who had set his omelet down.

In his mind's eye, she looked more and more like the woman on the beach.

He wished she would have said something that day.

"Yeah, there's some health issues in the family." Bill lifted his fedora and rubbed a hand over his thinning hair. "Some of us business owners are thinking about getting together and opening it for her, because she can't really afford to miss the tourist season, but we need to okay that with her. And no one has talked to her since she got some really bad news yesterday."

John nodded without saying anything. He'd given his share of bad news to people yesterday.

The mother with the son who only had a few months to live—being generous on the few months—was one of those that wouldn't leave his mind. She'd looked tragically devastated, although she also looked like she'd known the diagnosis was coming.

He hated giving them out. That was definitely one thing he was not going to miss about his job.

That mother yesterday had stirred in him some of the same feelings that the woman on the beach had.

He didn't allow personal feelings to mix with business and professional feelings, though.

He couldn't.

He saw too many people every single day. He had to admit sometimes their faces blurred together, but he always remembered the ones he gave a timeline to.

It felt a little like playing God when he estimated the amount of time a person had left.

It was a terrible feeling to estimate the time left for a child.

It was even more terrible to look into a parent's eyes while he did it.

Even though, if he were to meet that woman outside of the office, he might be pulled toward her, he couldn't allow any of those feelings to affect him inside the office.

He didn't have a problem being professional. Although, there were patients that he enjoyed seeing more than others.

Yesterday was one of those days, few and far between, where he wanted to take the woman in front of him into his arms and hold her.

Similar to the woman at the beach.

It had been a long time since he felt that feeling, and never as strong as yesterday.

"Is there a fundraiser or something I can donate to? I've been here before and really enjoyed it."

"Well, I guess we hadn't gotten that far, but there should be."

John reached into his pocket for the business card he always carried. He hardly ever gave them out, but there was one time he was exceptionally glad he had it—earlier this spring at the beach.

Not that she'd ever contacted him.

But he liked to think she could if she needed him.

He pulled the card out and handed it to Bill. "Contact me if you get something set up. I will donate, for sure." He saw again the slender woman with the plate in her hand and the ball cap pulled low, her hair coming out the hole in the back.

Hair that was very similar in length to the woman at the beach.

The lady yesterday had short hair.

Hair could be cut. Facial features didn't change as rapidly, but he hadn't been able to see features on the lady at the beach, even though he'd felt them, his face against hers, his mouth on her chin and down her neck. His forehead resting on hers as their breaths mingled and their bodies moved. He had forgotten nothing.

He didn't typically use his lips to recognize people. Ever.

Bill looked at the card, unlike the lady he'd given it to, and he looked back up. "You're a doctor?" he asked, surprise flooding his tone.

"That's right," John said.

"I would never have guessed that." Bill's eyes went up and down his outfit, similar to what he'd worn before, only it was warm enough that he went without the leggings and just wore shorts. "I'll be sure to let you know. I'm not sure when that'll be." The man's voice dipped low, out of either respect or true sorrow, John wasn't sure.

He wanted to ask what the medical issue was, and what the problems were, but that seemed too nosy for a complete stranger. He didn't want to come off like a stalker.

He didn't want to be a stalker.

The woman knew how to get a hold of him if she needed him. She hadn't. Maybe he should just accept that and move on.

But what they'd done sat hard on his conscience. While he didn't like that he'd done it, he also didn't like he couldn't shake the feelings he had for the woman. The desire to see her again was strong.

Maybe he just needed to look into her face and have her tell him that she didn't want him.

He didn't want that either, because even two months later, it still meant something to him.

He supposed he needed to hear from her that it hadn't meant anything to her in order for him to let it go. Even then, he probably wouldn't. He was the kind of man who stuck and stayed.

Once on a course, it was hard to change. For him anyway.

At times, he'd envied those men who could have two or three girls on the string or go from girl to girl without any trouble or second thoughts.

But truly, he didn't want to be like them, because that just wasn't who he was.

"I'd better get going," he said. "Thanks for coming over and talking to me. Appreciate it."

"Sure. Come on around when you're back in town, and hopefully she'll be open."

"I will." And he meant it.

Chapter 9

ANITRA STOOD IN HER son's room, staring at his small form looking so tiny in the big bed.

She hadn't said anything to him today either, despite the prognosis from the day before.

When she left the doctor's office, she got numbers for counselors, and when the first one didn't answer, she called the second.

They were from different groups, and she'd spoken with both of them today.

They had given her different advice.

One had told her to tell her son exactly what the doctor said and gave her several ways to comfort him.

The other had told her not to say anything and just let his physical abilities dictate what he did.

Both of them made sense.

If it were her, she'd want to know.

Probably.

Regardless, she hadn't said anything today, and they'd gone down and signed up for summer baseball.

Thankfully, practices didn't start until next week.

She supposed she'd have to make a decision then as to whether he could go to practice or not.

When they'd gotten back from the doctor's appointment, she'd flipped the closed sign on the window at the diner, told Iva May she could go ahead and go home, and went in and sat down, crying at the kitchen table while Jordan watched cartoons in the living room.

He hadn't even had the energy to play video games.

She didn't know how she was going to make it, but she wasn't going to try to keep the shop open and spend what could possibly be the last weeks of his life with her son.

If she lost him, *when* she lost him, it wouldn't matter if she had a shop or not.

Except it would. Her hand went to her stomach. She didn't just have Jordan to think about anymore.

Wiping her eyes, she went in and lay down on the couch with him, watching the mindless cartoons and wishing her idyllic time at the beach was her current reality.

Hours later, she carried her sleeping son to his room, tucking him in and kneeling at his bed, her head buried in the mattress next to his skinny shoulder and her tears dripping down into the sheets.

Finally, she wiped her face and tiptoed out of his room, coming face-to-face with Iva May. She hadn't heard her come in.

"There are a few of us downstairs in the shop. We were wondering if you would come down and talk to us for a minute?"

She nodded, putting an unconscious hand over her stomach.

Her little one in there, safe and warm for now, was the reason that she needed to be concerned about her shop.

She followed Iva May down and wondered if someone was maybe thinking that they could take it over for her.

But where would she live? She had the rooms behind and upstairs as her living quarters. They had been sufficient for Jordan and her, and so close to the lake, it felt like they had the whole beach as their backyard.

She didn't want to leave.

She walked into the small dining room of the diner. All the shop owners from up and down both sides of the street were there. And her mom and Iva May.

She couldn't help it. The tears that were never far from the surface overflowed her eyes again, from seeing everyone down in the shop, whether they were there to rent it from her or not.

Everyone, every single one, had come.

She didn't need to know why to appreciate that.

She sniffed and swallowed to try to make her throat stretch out so she could speak. "Thank you. I don't know why you're here, but thank you so much. So good to see all of you." And to know she wasn't alone.

She felt so lonely at times.

It was so good to know she wasn't alone.

Bill, who owned the surf shop down the street, put his hand up to get her attention and spoke when she looked at him. "We don't want to take up too much of your time. I know that time is precious right now. But we wanted to let you know we've all talked about it, and we will cover for your store, keeping it open, no matter what we have to do." He held both hands up and looked a little embarrassed. "I can't bake."

A couple of people laughed about that. Not loud laughter, but muted, out of respect.

"I can serve tables, wash dishes, sweep floors, and run the cash register if necessary. I'm also at the bank every day, and I don't mind making your deposits. Whatever it takes. We mean that."

Tears were flowing in earnest now, and she clung to Iva May and her mother, although her eyes swept the room and saw the heads nod in agreement.

She didn't deserve this. She knew everyone, of course. They all often congregated in the dining portion of her little diner, but she'd never gotten too far involved in anyone's business before.

"You're one of us. We'll take care of you," said Teagan, who was young and single and owned the virtual video store up the street.

There were nods and murmurs of agreement.

Then Beverly Ellis stood up. She had left Blueberry Beach as soon as she graduated from high school and had gone on to college and become very successful in some sort of business. Anitra wasn't even sure exactly what her business entailed, but she'd semi-retired and come back. She was the reason they had a hospital. She'd donated almost exclusively to build the trauma center.

Anitra figured she probably was behind the oncology unit that had opened as well.

She was dressed simply in a short-sleeved sweater that emphasized her slimness and dress slacks, both in neutral colors. She moved with grace as she walked forward, taking Anitra's hand.

"Don't worry about your lease. I've talked to the landlord, and I'll be paying it for the next year. I know everyone's keeping your shop open, and I hope that that will be enough to give you some money to go away with your son if you need to. Or afterwards..." Her voice trailed off, like she didn't want to say what she did, but it needed to be said.

Anitra stepped away from her mother and Iva May and took Beverly's proffered hands. "You don't have to walk around on tenterhooks with me. I know I'm a mess right now. I'm getting used to the diagnosis, and I don't want this to be a sad time. I mean..." She let out a breath.

She didn't want people to think she wasn't grieving for her son. Because she was. And she would.

"I just know that he's going to be in a better place. I know God has a plan. As much as sometimes I just hate to even think that when God has hard things in his plan, I have to go through them, I know they'll be good for me. And for Jordan. I'm just gonna trust the Lord to get me through this. So don't feel like you can't laugh when you're around me. Because," she looked around the room, as sincere as she could be, "I need it. I need to laugh. I need your smiles. And I'm so blessed by what you're offering to do."

Bill shifted. "If you have a specific way you want us to operate, let us know. Otherwise, we'll figure it out for ourselves. Although we do promise we won't serve anything that's burnt to patrons, we can't guarantee that it will always taste as good as yours."

Anitra appreciated his humor, and even though his voice was lowered, she was glad that he wasn't being completely solemn and serious.

"Thank you. However you handle it is fine."

She had certain things that she did and ways that she did things, but she wasn't going to micromanage people who were here to help her and who weren't expecting anything in return. Because they knew she didn't have anything to give.

"I have recipes. I'll print them out and put them in the kitchen." She looked at Iva May, who stood off to the side, leaning against the counter. "Iva May knows how to order supplies from my distributor. She knows pretty much everything. She can run it herself."

There were some titters at that last, and then everyone gathered around her, offering their support, and sympathy, and anything they had that she might need.

"I think some of your regular customers will want to contribute. If you don't mind, we'll set up a jar or something for them to donate. Or maybe we'll set something up online. I already have one person who volunteered and asked where he could donate." Bill spoke from the table that he always sat at. It made her smile that he would sit at the same place even during a meeting. Like an old cow going to the same stanchion every time.

She stayed down with her friends and neighbors for more than an hour and a half before walking slowly back up to her apartment.

She was heartbroken and didn't have words for the sorrow about Jordan, but she'd been so blessed by her friends. It didn't begin to make up for losing her son, of course, but she could see that God was giving her a rainbow in her clouds. And she made sure to thank him for it.

The next day, she decided to do what she thought was best for her son, and she sat down at the kitchen table and had a long talk with him. She told him exactly what the doctor had said and exactly what he could expect.

And true to her gut, he didn't seem very upset.

His big eyes were solemn. "I had a dream about heaven last night. God has a baseball team. I get to play on it. I'm going to be the pitcher. And He's gonna show me how to improve my swing. I'm gonna be the best batter in heaven."

All right, so that made Anitra's nose prick, and her eyes fill up, but she was tired of crying, and she didn't want to do it in front of her son, not when he was being so happy.

She didn't want to make him sad because she was sad.

So she smiled her plastic smile. "That's fantastic. I didn't realize there was a baseball team in heaven. I guess...you win every game?"

He shrugged his shoulders like it didn't matter. "I don't care. All I want to do is play. And I want to run faster too. Jesus said when I get to heaven, I'll run a lot faster. He also said it wouldn't hurt anymore."

Either he didn't care that he wasn't going to be seeing his mother in heaven or the thought hadn't occurred to him yet.

She didn't care, and she wasn't going to point it out.

"It sounds like you have everything settled then."

"Yep." His face fell a little. "Jesus said there's no video games in heaven. Can I go play some now?"

There was a long pause before she managed to get a word out. "Sure."

She watched as he got up, gingerly, like the pain was getting worse.

Hospice was supposed to be coming today, and she'd been told they would help with that. She hoped so. She couldn't have asked for Jordan to have a better attitude, and as long as he wasn't hurting, having things go this well with him would help her.

She didn't even go down to the store that day. She assumed it was open, but she didn't know.

There was a nagging thought in the back of her head, that she didn't deserve what everyone was doing for her. If they knew what she had done, and eventually it was going to come out, they would be disappointed in her.

She had a hard time dealing with the guilt, so she went in and asked Jordan if she could play with him.

He was happy to have her, and she was happy to spend some time with her son.

Still, after she put him to bed, a combination of the guilt, and maybe the hormones too, and of course the grief, had her sitting at the kitchen table, crying.

A short rap on her door before it opened didn't give her enough time to wipe her eyes and hide the evidence.

"Oh, honey," Iva May said as she walked in, closing the door behind her. "I'm so sorry."

Anitra shook her head. "I'm fine, really. I'm sad, of course, but not sad enough to sit here and cry."

"Of course you are. That's what you're doing."

How could she tell Iva May about the guilt that ate at her?

"If people knew how bad I was, they wouldn't help me. It makes me feel guilty."

"Now you stop that," Iva May said, sitting down and putting an arm around her. "You're not any worse than anybody else."

"But you don't know what I've done!" Anitra cried.

"I guarantee you that whatever you've done is no worse than what anyone else has done." Her hand clasped Anitra's. "We all have secrets."

"You don't. Everyone knows everything about you, and you're perfect." Maybe it wasn't true that she was completely perfect, but it felt like it.

"No. I guarantee you I have skeletons in my closet as well. Things I don't ever want anyone to find out." Iva May looked as sincere as anyone Anitra had ever seen.

Anitra looked, with new eyes, at Iva May. What in the world could be so terrible that she didn't want anyone to find it out?

It couldn't be any worse than her own secret. She put a hand over her stomach. It seemed to be an automatic reaction, protecting the little one inside.

"And if you're talking about the baby you're carrying? I already know." Iva May's kind eyes held compassion as she took Anitra's hand in both of her old and wrinkled yet soft and warm ones.

Anitra couldn't contain her surprise. She'd thought she'd been very secretive. "How did you know? I haven't told anyone. I haven't even gone to the doctor yet."

She'd been taking store-bought prenatal vitamins. She wanted everything to be perfect with her baby, and thankfully, she hadn't had any trouble other than the normal morning sickness.

"Well, I think it's a mother's instinct to put a hand over her stomach especially when she's pregnant. But I have watched Jordan a lot, and I saw the pregnancy test box in the garbage can. Not that I go through your trash," Iva May said, closing her eyes for a minute. "But it was just sitting there on the top. I knew there was a possibility. That, combined with the fact that you've been sick off and on for the last couple months, especially in the morning. I work with you in the morning, remember? I had my suspicions." Iva May rubbed her hand. "Don't worry. I'm not going to tell anyone. That's your information to either keep close or let go."

She loved the way Iva May said that. It was true; she was keeping that information close. She wasn't ready to let it out to the world, even though it would soon not be her choice. She was wearing clothes that were slightly looser already.

She didn't look pregnant yet, but her waist was thickening. Soon she would.

"Thank you. I...I just feel overwhelmed."

"As well you should." Iva May hesitated. "Did you ever get the money back from your ex?"

"No. My lawyer is working on it, but I know it's probably going to cost me about as much as he took in order to get it back. If I do. But it's the principle of the thing. He's taken so much from me already, I'm not going to let him have another penny." Or thought, she added to herself.

In order to do that, she had to shove the thoughts that wanted to crowd into her head out.

She wanted to be angry, and bitter, and hate him.

She wanted to look him up on the internet and see what he was doing. If he ever actually married the woman he was with, or whether he left her too.

Either one wouldn't surprise her.

Regardless whether he married her now, he'd leave her later.

She wished she'd have seen what a snake he was before she got wrapped up in him. She wished she hadn't spent years hoping he would change or hoping she would somehow be good enough to keep him.

For Jordan's sake.

All of those were things she wanted, but if she wasn't going to waste any more brainpower on him, then she needed to let it all go.

"Has he been around to see his son?" Iva May asked carefully.

Anitra pursed her lips. That was the thing she really couldn't think about. She would get angry and be miserable all day.

"No." She made a conscious effort to keep the anger out of her tone and to make it pleasant. She was somewhat successful.

"He's a jerk, and he doesn't deserve your time," Iva May said with uncharacteristic heat.

That little glimpse of emotion under her normally sweet old lady exterior intrigued Anitra.

She'd rather think about Iva May, and what secret she could be hiding, than her own life.

"Are you ever going to tell anyone your secret?"

Iva May shook her head. "My secret is the kind of secret that will change people's lives, and not in a good way, and I could get in trouble for it, and people would hate me."

Anitra wanted to ask why. She wanted to ask for more, but she needed to respect Iva May's privacy as Iva May had respected hers.

"If you ever need someone to talk to about it, I owe you more than I can repay," she finally said, feeling like it wasn't enough but not having anything to offer Iva May except herself and her confidence.

"It took place a long time ago. Decades. And sometimes those secrets have a tendency to haunt you, but mine worked out for the best. I think. I know the Lord's going to have something to say to me when I stand in front of him. I'm not looking forward to it." Iva May gave Anitra's hand one last tap before she straightened and stood. "Can I do anything for you, child?" she asked softly.

"No. Thank you. It was good to see you tonight. You snapped me out of my crying jag."

Iva May smiled. "I know your mother would like to be here, but she can't afford to close her salon any more than you can afford to close your diner."

"I know. And she's done so much for me already."

"Do you want to take a walk?" Iva May asked.

"Not tonight. But thank you. Maybe soon. Maybe..." She didn't say after Jordan passed away, although that's what she was thinking. Of course, at that point, she didn't need anyone to come and sit at her house so that she could go walk on the beach.

At that point, she'd need to start preparing for the new little one.

Chapter 10

JOHN WALKED UP FROM the beach as the sun was just peeking over the horizon.

He determined that he was going to come here every day for his jog, regardless of his schedule.

He wasn't so invaluable that the hospital couldn't live without him until nine o'clock in the morning.

He didn't have patients he was seeing anymore, didn't have rounds to make, and was solely overseeing the transition team.

It upset him more than he could say that the little café was closed.

He'd hoped to get another glimpse of the woman. Even if it wasn't the one from the beach, maybe it was her sister. Maybe she would know about her. Maybe he would think of something to ask.

Even worse was the idea that maybe the illness in the family was the woman he met.

He wasn't in the habit of worrying over things. Normally, he was able to shut his brain down and compartmentalize. Thinking about a problem when he had time and putting it aside when he didn't.

But concern about the woman had leaked into other areas of his life.

He thought about her yesterday while he was seeing patients, and while he was in a meeting with the transition team, and while he had been reading up on the latest experimental trials. Looking for something for that mother that he hadn't been able to get out of his mind. For her son.

He hadn't found anything. In fact, for the type of cancer the boy had, he hadn't found any hope at all. Especially with the way it was growing.

Even though he wasn't expecting the café to be open, he still walked up the street, deep in thought.

He was almost in front of it before he realized that the bright neon sign was flashing "OPEN."

Chuckling a little at himself that all of his worries were unfounded, he opened the door and walked in.

It was early yet, but there were still several people filling up tables and two standing in line.

He walked over and became the third.

Just a few seconds later, Bill, of all people, walked out of the kitchen with a white apron tied around his waist and two plates in his hands.

When Bill saw him, the older man almost smiled. His eyes definitely lit up.

John nodded in greeting.

His eyes dropped to the plates in Bill's hands, and he thought maybe the blobs on them were supposed to be omelets, but they didn't have the bright yellow, greens, and reds that he typically associated with an omelet.

They looked like a watery brownish color.

Not very appetizing.

Maybe the woman who had been in the back really wasn't there.

Bill walked back in the kitchen without saying anything. The two people in front of him ordered and moved off.

The same gray-haired woman was running the cash register, and John placed the same order he had every time he'd come in.

The woman didn't seem quite as cheerful this morning, and she did nothing more than comment about the weather. He replied with something equally uninspired, paid, then went and sat down.

He had an article from a medical journal that had just been released that he wanted to look at, so he got his phone out while he was waiting.

It wasn't long until Bill set a plate with a not very appetizing egg white omelet down in front of him.

"I'm sorry it's not better. I never was a very good cook."

"You're cooking?" John had assumed Bill was just maybe...waiting tables? He hadn't thought he was actually making the food, although that explained why it was brownish rather than white. Although if he couldn't cook, it opened up a whole slew of new questions.

"Sure am. Everyone around here's pitching in for Anitra."

Anitra. Nice name. A little unusual, but he'd had a patient with that name not long ago if he remembered correctly.

It seemed familiar, but he wasn't pulling a face. Since the patients were technically his but were going to be assigned to one of his team members, he didn't know them quite as well as he normally did his own.

Anitra.

"Well, I suppose practice makes perfect," he said, looking at the eggs and thinking it was going to take an awful lot of practice before they were perfect.

"If you happen to know anyone who has a couple of hours in the morning and who can make good omelets, we're hiring. The pay's not great, but the company is." Bill kind of did a little thing with sticking his chest out, like he was the company.

John allowed a small smile to tweak his lips up. "I cook a mean omelet." He surprised himself with that statement. What was he trying to do? Was he offering to cook omelets?

"Well, you're welcome to come back and audition. Got orders for two more," Bill said.

"The cook delivers the omelets?"

"We do whatever we need to around here," Bill said, turning slightly. "If you need anything else, let me know."

He walked away, and John sat in his seat for ten more seconds before he stood.

The girl he was looking for was local. He'd seen someone in this diner that put him in mind of her. He wanted to find her.

Even if that weren't all true, he might have stood up anyway.

He'd worked twelve- to sixteen-hour days for a long time, and while he loved being a doctor, he didn't want that to be the only thing that he did with his life.

He didn't want to look back one day and wish he had a wife and a family and friends outside of the hospital and something that he could point to that he had done, aside from staying within the sterile walls of the hospital and handing out diagnoses and treatment plans and...giving parents an estimation of the time their child had left on this earth.

He wanted...not more exactly but just wanted to step aside and breathe a little, maybe.

Standing, he took his coffee in one hand, shoved his phone under his arm, and picked up his plate. He followed the path that Bill had taken and went back to the kitchen.

Two hours later, an apron wrapped around his waist, dirty from wiping his hands on it for the last two hours, John had cooked more than he'd cooked in his life before.

But he'd also had fun.

Bill seemed kind of crotchety and grumpy, but it actually hid a great sense of humor, and John really liked him.

Not to mention, any man who owned a surf shop but would come over and help his neighboring business associate in their kitchen, making omelets, was a man who deserved respect in his book.

John had learned the lady's name who worked behind the cash register was Iva May, and she came to carry out plates as well.

When they were both busy, he carried them out himself.

He actually kind of liked it, looking at the tourists and having them look at him and think he actually belonged here when he didn't belong any more than they did.

Except, he'd moved here. He expected to put down roots here. He hadn't bought a house yet, but he was renting a small cottage outside of town and was looking for a place.

If he didn't find one, he'd build. But he didn't really want the hassle and was content to stay at his cottage and wait for the right place to go on the market.

Still, he intended to stay.

Winters here couldn't be that much worse than winters in Chicago. And if he wasn't going to be at the hospital all day, he could imagine being cozied up by the fire, writing his manuscript, and...maybe the woman from the beach would be in that picture somehow. As his wife? As his date? As his girlfriend?

He felt like he might be a little old for a girlfriend, but he'd take her with whatever title he could get her.

Maybe he would end up not liking her. Or she would end up not liking him, but he wanted to be able to try.

When he unwrapped his apron and looked around for a place to put it, Bill came over.

"Thanks a lot for your help. I think we can handle it from here. Sometimes, it gets busy around lunch, but we'll figure it out.

"You coming in tomorrow?" Bill asked, kinda casually, but his gaze was shrewd.

"I...I had thought of it." Why not? He had every plan in the world of getting up and going for a jog; he could get up a little earlier and be done with his run when the diner opened. "You open at five?"

Bill's shrewd look melted into a grin. "That's right. If you want to come a little earlier, get the griddle hot, you can. But I'll be here. Iva May will too."

"I'll be here before five."

John heard the bit of disbelief in his voice, there for good reason.

He could not believe he had just said that he would show up at the diner before five and cook omelets until eight.

But he couldn't think of another thing that would be more beneficial for him to do. And he hadn't had a terrible time. It was different than the work that he normally did and relaxing in a way.

"Should I take this home and wash it myself?" he asked, holding up his apron.

"Yeah. If you do that..." Bill untied his and handed it over. "If you wouldn't mind washing mine too, that'd be great."

John stood there, holding the aprons, bemused. Really?

Bill grinned, and John had to return it.

"That's fine. I'll do them today, you do them tomorrow?"

"That's a deal," Bill said easily with another grin as he sauntered off.

John shook his head. He was going to like it here. A lot different than the hospital atmosphere. A little more welcoming, a lot warmer, definitely more casual.

It smelled better too.

The hope that his beach lady might show up at any time was a little bit of excitement that sent a buzz through his body and gave him an edge.

He liked working with an edge.

It had been a while since he'd been excited about his work and felt this sense of anticipation. Maybe he was burned out.

Chapter 11

ANITRA STOOD, STRAIGHT and still, her mother on one side, the casket containing the remains of her son on the other.

Her husband had not come to visit at all. He hadn't seen Jordan for months before he was diagnosed with this last round of cancer.

Anitra prayed that he didn't come to the funeral. He had every right in the world to come, of course, but the one dim spot in the last few weeks, other than Jordan's impending departure from this world, was the fact that his father didn't come see him.

Anitra didn't give a flip for herself, but anything that hurt her son hurt her as well, and this made her angry.

It wouldn't have been that hard. It wasn't like Danny lived on the other side of the world.

He could have made the drive from Ann Arbor.

But he hadn't.

Jordan had never made it to any baseball practices.

Hospice had been wonderful. They'd kept his pain managed, and he had very few days where he was exceptionally uncomfortable.

Some of the kids from his class had come to see him while he was still alive, and like little kids, they were uncomfortable, but they'd been sweet. They'd brightened Jordan's days.

Anitra had thanked their mothers profusely for bringing them.

She'd been equally impressed with the father who had brought his little girl in.

He'd seemed as uncomfortable as the boys who visited Jordan. But his daughter had been sweet and had stayed with Jordan longer than any of the other kids.

It made Anitra's heart twist to see her sit beside Jordan's bedside, her little hand slipping slowly across the covers until it covered his.

Jordan's hand had turned, and their fingers had linked, and Anitra had to turn away.

Her son wouldn't know romance. Wouldn't have a girlfriend. Would never grow up, get married, and have children.

Even though it had worked out terribly for her, that was probably one of her biggest regrets, that he would miss all that.

Because love could be so sweet.

Just because she'd had a bad deal didn't mean that there wasn't such a thing as a lifetime love.

Those were the things she couldn't think about.

It would be hard to go home to her empty apartment with his things still there. To walk into his room and look at his bed, to see the posters of baseball players that he had on those walls, to see his glove and his favorite bat. His clothes.

But she was going to need to do something, because she had to get a nursery ready for the baby.

She could give herself a few months. It wasn't urgent.

"You can do this, honey." Her mother squeezed her hand and looked over at her.

It was almost time for the church doors to open, and there were people standing outside already.

She probably couldn't get through it without crying, but that was her goal.

One of the men from the mortuary, a local man that she'd grown up with, Tom, opened the church doors, and people walked slowly in.

The next couple hours were a blur as she spoke with people, some she knew, some she really didn't.

People walked by, one face blending into the next as they hugged her and said a few words about Jordan. His friends from school, their parents, and his teachers.

People who would be continuing to raise their children and doing all the normal things that parents expected to do with them, including getting their driver's license, first dates, and graduation from high school and college.

Things she would never do with Jordan.

She focused her thoughts on each person in front of her and tried to smile and let them know that they didn't need to be sad. Not for her, and not for Jordan either.

Death was a natural part of living, and although his had come too early, it had come at the exact right time. The Lord had a plan. She had to have faith in that, even when it wavered.

By the time it was over, hours after it was scheduled to be, and she was able to sit down, her feet ached along with her back, and her throat hurt from holding back tears.

She'd been almost successful in her goal, and she really wanted to be alone.

"Do you want me to go home with you?" her mother asked. Her eyes were concerned, her forehead wrinkled.

"No. Not unless you need to. You've been better to me than I deserve. I know you've lost business because of it. I'll be fine. I'll let you know if I need anything."

Her mother walked out the door with her arm around her.

Her feet dragged. Her heart scratched at her back, not wanting to go. She couldn't shake the feeling that she was leaving her son behind no matter how hard she tried to convince herself it was just his body. Jordan was no longer on earth, no longer with her.

He was playing baseball in heaven.

Chapter 12

"ARE YOU COMING TO THE viewing tonight?" Bill asked as John stood in the kitchen, expertly sprinkling vegetables over the egg white in the large skillet.

He'd heard that Anitra's son had passed.

He hadn't met Anitra, hadn't seen her.

From what he understood, she spent every last moment with her son who was dying of cancer.

He wondered if he was a patient in his oncology unit.

But the chances were small. From what little he'd been able to gather, she'd been in Chicago under the care of an oncologist he recognized there.

Whether or not her son's case had been transferred so late in its term, he didn't know.

It always made him think about the woman that he'd seen—the first one in the new oncology unit. The one that had left such an impression on him.

He'd only seen her once.

He'd ordered hospice for her son.

They hadn't been part of his caseload in Chicago, and he wouldn't have remembered them at all, except the woman had reminded him of the lady on the beach.

He hadn't seen that lady at all in the six weeks he'd been working in the diner.

Not that he would recognize her if he did.

He was afraid he wouldn't. He didn't know how he would figure it out. Or what he was expecting, being here.

Still, he made a point of walking on the beach at sunset if he could.

Most of the time, he was working late, but he definitely did it on Saturday and Sunday nights. He hadn't run into her.

He figured he might as well give up and maybe turn his attention to someone else.

He hadn't been able to.

"So, is this really a hard question that deserves that much thought, or did you forget I'm here?"

John shook his head and looked up from the skillet at Bill who was waving his hand in front of his eyes. "Sorry. I spaced out." He looked back down at the skillet. The omelet was ready to turn. "Give me some room. There's a knack to turning these things."

"That would be terrible if we got a complaint. You've only had two since you started."

"I know. I don't even want to have one."

"It's the doctor coming out in you." Ever since Bill had found out he was a doctor, he blamed everything that went wrong on it.

"I guess. There shouldn't be any reason to complain about this one," he said as he flattened it with a spatula, then scooted it out of the skillet and put it on a plate. "You doing the honors?"

"Yeah. Might as well. Although, I know you enjoy it." Bill smirked before picking up the plate and walking through the swinging doors.

John grabbed the next order and started on it, smiling to himself.

Bill was fun to work with, and he enjoyed it. Bill was also right; he liked carrying the plates out to the customers. Once in a while, one of them recognized him as Dr. Chambers, but most of them just knew him as John.

He liked that.

Bill came back in and worked on making toast and a fruit cup, grabbing some blueberries and yogurt out of the refrigerator. "So, did you make a decision about that viewing?"

"I don't know her, but I've been working in her diner for over a month and a half now. I guess I should go."

He didn't typically make a habit of going to his own patients' funerals. Sometimes, seeing him wasn't comforting to the parents. Sometimes, they got angry. There were families who blamed him for their child's death. That he didn't do enough or soon enough or maybe they were just angry and grieving and needed to lash out at someone.

Sometimes, parents invited him, and he always tried to go to those. It was an honor that people thought so much of him that they wanted him at the celebration of life for their child. He liked those the best.

"I thought it would be nice. I don't know if she knows who all is down here or not, but it would be great to support her." Bill scooped some yogurt out as his toast popped up. "I know this last whole year has been extremely difficult for her. She's a nice lady and deserves a lot better than what she's been given." Bill slapped butter on the toast and threw the fruit cup on a plate beside it like an old hand.

"Her husband's dead?" John asked, since as far as he knew the man hadn't been around. He'd heard a little bit of gossip, but he had to hand it to Iva May; she wasn't a gossiper.

"No. He cheated on her for a while before he finally left her. Bounced from woman to woman before he found one he wanted to stick with, or got her pregnant anyway, and finally demanded a divorce, shortly before Jordan's cancer came back. Like I said, Anitra's had a tough time of it."

That stunk. He'd heard his share of sob stories, though.

Not that he'd gotten calloused by them or anything, but that really was the way life was. Sometimes, it just wasn't fair. Sometimes, it was downright ugly.

Bill rattled off the name of the church and the time, and John nodded his head.

Bill didn't usually hold onto things quite like he had, and John could only assume the older man wanted him to go.

So he would.

When he walked into the church that night, it was crowded. The line going to the casket was long and wound out of the church and down around the corner.

John slipped in and stood in the back.

There were chairs full of people, children, and adults. Many sniffling and some outright crying and sobbing.

A woman, younger than him, stood at the head of the casket flanked by an older woman. Her mother maybe.

He looked at the younger woman and tried to reconcile her as the owner of the diner where he had been working in the mornings for the last six weeks.

As he studied the woman, he was pretty sure she was the one who had been in his office, shortly after they opened.

He was terrible at recognizing people, but she gave him the same feeling that that woman did.

Even though she seemed a little heavier than that woman had been.

Disappointment settled in his stomach, because definitely she wasn't the woman at the beach, since the woman at the beach was almost painfully thin.

Not that he could tell when she was standing up with her loose tunic dress on.

It was because of what they'd done later.

This woman wore a blouse tucked into a knee-length black skirt. It wasn't hard to discern that, although she wasn't fat, she was much more padded around the middle than the lady at the beach.

Still, she gave him that same indescribable feeling.

She was probably the woman who had set his food down at the table in the diner. The one with the cap pulled low. She'd given him the same feeling.

Protective feelings stirred inside of him. He hadn't been expecting that, since he didn't even know her.

Although he'd been working now for a while to help her keep her business afloat so she'd have something to go back to once things settled down.

He'd enjoyed the work, but he'd been doing it for her.

Not that someone ever got over the death of a child. He didn't think it was possible. There just was a hole where there used to be a heart.

He stood in the back, never going to the casket. He wasn't sure how this woman would react to seeing the doctor who had told her there was no hope.

Eventually, Bill made it through the line and came back and stood beside him for a bit before they turned in silence.

John left with the odd feeling never resolved and with a heavy heart as well. The woman seemed nice, and as Bill had pointed out, she certainly didn't deserve the hand life had dealt her.

Chapter 13

JOHN SET THE EGGBEATER aside and poured the eggs into the skillet. He loved the sound of the sizzle.

It might seem simple, especially after all his years of medical school, residency, and training, but working at the diner had been relaxing and very good for his stress levels.

The transition at the hospital had gone mostly well, but there was just something about coming in here where all he needed to focus on was making a good omelet. No one was going to die, no one was crying, he didn't have to hand anybody tissues.

Except, the whole time he'd been working here, he had been very aware that the lady upstairs was losing her son.

That had been the only wrinkle in his happiness.

The work here made him a better doctor. Just taking this time to run as the sun came up on his right and the water reflected on his left, and then he came in and cooked and chatted with tourists and regulars.

He had been enjoying it.

"Are you coming to the funeral today?" Bill asked as he brought a stack of dirty dishes in and set them at the sink where a teenage boy was scraping them off.

"I kinda wanted to. Do you think it's all right?"

"'Course. Why wouldn't it be all right?"

John looked over his shoulder, then back to where he was spreading vegetables over the top of the omelet. "I don't know. There were a lot of people there last night. I hate to take up the room. I'm not exactly a good friend."

"I think anyone who can go and support her is welcome. I'm sure there is space for everyone."

John nodded. Bill didn't say anything more.

He'd gone to the viewing by himself, although he'd met Bill there. As old as he was, and having been single all his life, he was used to going places by himself. Or just not going.

It wasn't that.

It was the interest that he felt in Anitra was inappropriate. Not inappropriate in general but inappropriate at this time in her life. Not at a viewing, and not at a funeral.

He'd need to hang back again.

Or use his professional demeanor to make sure that he was very, very appropriate.

He didn't typically have trouble with being inappropriate.

Thoughts of the beach lady rolled through his mind again. A soft breeze. A light touch along his jaw. Whispered words and a gentle smile.

He could remember everything.

But in the six weeks he'd worked here, she hadn't been in that he knew of, and he hadn't seen her on the beach any night he'd been, which had been as often as he could. Every weekend, and at least half the weekdays.

His time on the beach had been profitable for at least one thing: any property that he looked at was going to have beach frontage.

He'd already cleared it with the hospital to be off today, although he still went in and worked until 10:30.

He would be pushing it to make it on time, and he almost didn't go.

He'd be showing up late enough that anyone who was a good friend of the family would have the best seats, and he'd take what was left.

He drove to the church. The lot was full. He ended up parking at the public beach parking, which was full as well, but he managed to find a spot as someone left.

The funeral was already started when he walked in. He stood in the back, with the rest of the overflow crowd, and listened as the pastor talked about Jordan's last days, and Jordan playing baseball in heaven, and Anitra.

He thought maybe she'd speak, but she didn't. The pastor just talked about her faith and how she wanted people to be happy rather than sad, since Jordan was with the Lord and running around, pain free.

He picked her out at the front, sitting straight, not moving. Her hair was up, some kind of bun, with little tendrils trailing around her neck, which was graceful and slender.

It made him think of his beach lady, and he had to look away, focusing instead on the Scriptures and the short message the pastor brought.

By 11:30, it was over, and the people trailed out. He stayed where he was, nodding at the ones who nodded and smiled at him, waiting.

More than an hour later, everyone had filed out, and Anitra spoke with the pastor alone at the front.

The older lady who had stood at the casket with her last night walked out of the sanctuary, looked at him, did a double-take, and walked over.

"I'm Glenna Richardson," she said, holding out her hand. "I'm Anitra's mother, Jordan's grandmother."

"I'm John," he said simply.

"I think you're the doctor that we saw at the new Blueberry Beach Hospital oncology department the one time we were there with Jordan."

"That's right."

Her brows puckered like she didn't quite understand how one meeting would cause him to feel like he should come to the funeral, but she still said, "It was kind of you to come."

"I know I only saw Jordan once..." he started, knowing what he was going to say would sound crazy. "But I've actually been working in the diner. I've heard people talk about you helping your daughter, but I don't think we've met outside of the hospital."

Her eyes got big, and it was easy to see he surprised her. Of course. No one expected the head doctor of the oncology team to be flipping omelets at seven o'clock in the morning in a small lakeside town.

"Oh my goodness. You're John. The omelet man."

He had to grin at that. "Yep. That's me."

"Well, I'll be." She grunted a disbelieving puff of air. "I had no idea. I know Anitra doesn't either."

John put up a hand. "Maybe you don't need to tell her now. It's not that it's a big secret. I just didn't want any fanfare. I've actually been enjoying it."

Mrs. Richardson nodded, her eyes wise. "I think I understand. There's no pressure when you're coming in and making omelets for someone. I mean, other than don't burn them." She smiled a little. "It's not like the job you have at the hospital."

"Right. I'm stepping back a little in my role there too, but it has been a nice stress relief. I appreciate the opportunity."

"I know Anitra appreciated everyone pitching in. I don't know what she would have done without everyone. I'm sure you know, from being at the diner, that shop owners up and down the street have donated their time to keeping her little café open."

"I do. I can see that it's to their benefit to keep the diner going. People are more inclined to shop if they're not hungry."

"That's true," Mrs. Richardson said, her smile small. "Well. I won't say anything to Anitra, unless she asks of course. Can't lie."

"I would never ask you to." He hesitated but decided his next question was okay. "Do you have more than one daughter?" he asked kind of slowly, with a bit of hesitation.

"No. Anitra is all God gave me." Her face held sadness. "Jordan was all God gave Anitra. I wish He would have given her more. It would have made things harder, but maybe now she would have companionship. As it is, I feel bad for her going back to her apartment, alone."

He nodded, his heart drooping. He had almost been convinced that the beach lady was related to Anitra somehow. But she couldn't be.

Unless...

"You're from Blueberry Beach?" he asked.

"Yes. I am, my husband too, although he died in a construction accident when Anitra was small, and she never really knew him."

"You have family here?"

Now her eyes narrowed slightly, and he knew he'd overstepped. He shouldn't be that interested, but he thought maybe Anitra had a cousin.

"I'm asking because I met a lady on the beach, who reminds me some of Anitra. I wondered if she might be related. I never got her name."

"No. Anitra has cousins, but none of them live in Blueberry Beach. It's a small town, although maybe with the hospital, it will grow some."

He nodded. It almost certainly would. There were lots of doctors and nurses moving into the area who would have money to spend. Not to mention patients would need places to stay and shop.

"It's a beautiful town, and the beach is gorgeous. Especially at sunset." He shouldn't have said that. It brought images of a billowing dress and blowing hair and the feeling of a hand trailing down his back.

"Thank you. You're staying?"

"Yes. I'm renting a house right now, but I'm looking for beachfront property. I've been jogging on the beach every morning before going to the diner, and I've gotten quite fond of watching the sunrise reflect on the water. The sunsets are even better, as it disappears beyond the horizon. I love it here."

"Wait until July when the blueberries are ripe. Beach, beauty, blueberries. You can't beat it." Mrs. Richardson nodded firmly.

He had a feeling she was right.

"I assume you must be waiting because you want to talk to Anitra. I'll go ahead and wait out in the car. You can let her know."

He hadn't really been thinking that, although he supposed that was the obvious conclusion, since Mrs. Richardson and Anitra and the pastor were the only ones left in the church.

Mrs. Richardson turned and walked out the door as Anitra shook the pastor's hand and nodded one more time. He turned and walked to the side of the sanctuary, exiting through a door, which John imagined probably went to his office.

Anitra turned and ran her hand along the casket.

He supposed there were pallbearers somewhere waiting to take it. It had been announced that there would be no graveside service.

He took a few steps and stopped at the entrance of the sanctuary.

Wherever the pallbearers were, they were discreetly out of sight, and after sweeping the large room, his eyes rested on the woman at the casket.

He imagined it was hard to walk away. It probably felt like leaving your child. There was just some parenting instinct that wouldn't allow a parent to walk away from their child, putting them in the hands of a stranger for eternity.

It'd been hard enough, watching parents watch their child be wheeled away into surgery.

More than one had tried to grab a hold of the gurney and stop it or walk along with it.

Of all the times for parents to fall apart, that was the one. When their child was taken from them.

Even the news that their child had cancer, while shocking and sure to be upsetting, didn't elicit the strong emotions that having to stand and watch their child be taken from them did.

How much harder it must be to walk away herself.

He stood at the entrance, not leaning, just his hands hanging down at his sides, wishing he had strength or something to offer her as she said goodbye for the last time.

It was just a body in a casket. He knew it and she knew it, but it represented her responsibility for the last decade.

The narrow shoulders drew upward shakily and then wobbled as they went back down.

She was sobbing without any noise.

He typically wasn't the kind of person to hesitate, and he didn't at that point either.

Striding forward, he walked to the front and put his arm around those shoulders.

They felt familiar and right.

Funny that they would feel exactly like his beach woman, and yet, Anitra couldn't be his beach woman.

Could she?

"Miss Anitra," he said. He didn't want her to turn and realize it was a stranger holding her. But he couldn't not offer comfort.

She whirled quickly, her eyes wide, tears on her cheeks but confusion and shock on her face. Like she had recognized him somehow.

If she recognized him from his voice, from the one time he'd had an appointment with her, she had an extremely good ear.

He felt that was impossible.

Unless...

Chapter 14

ANITRA TURNED, KNOWING that it was Dr. John Chambers before she saw him.

The hand felt right, the scent of some type of sandalwood and strength familiar.

She hadn't had time to wipe her tears off her face, and she didn't have the presence of mind to try to not look shocked. To not look like she recognized him.

Immediately, suspicion entered his eyes, and if she hadn't already been wondering if it was her stupidity that had caused Jordan's death, she would be castigating herself because she'd allowed this man to know that she recognized his voice.

How could she not?

Even now, with all of the things that had happened, he sent shivers down her spine and warmth through her chest and brought back rich memories of sweet heat and gentle consideration.

Unique in her experience.

She didn't want those memories, not now. She didn't want this man. Not now.

No matter how good the memories, the experience had been wrong.

And now, she had to walk away from her son for the last time, and she was finding it harder than she expected.

"In the hospital, I'm not a surgeon, but the hardest thing for parents to do, ever, is to allow their child to be wheeled away from them, usually for surgery. There's just something in your parent DNA that can't stand to let your child out of your sight and leave them in the hands of strangers." His voice was exactly how she remembered. It soothed her in the deepest part of her soul and made her long to lean into him.

He had said exactly what she was feeling. How could she leave her little boy? She should stay beside him, guarding, protecting, loving. That was her job. That's what was assigned to her the moment she'd known she was expecting. From that second, it was her job to nurture and protect and love.

He understood that better than anyone else had. At least, he articulated it better.

Her mom had never lost a child, so as much as she wanted to be a support and encouragement, she just didn't understand.

Especially not about this.

Even though his eyes had narrowed with suspicion, she didn't think he recognized her.

Did it matter?

She decided not to care. She could only hurt so much, and right now, her broken heart was demanding all of her attention.

"Thank you for saying that. It helps. That's exactly how I feel."

He nodded, his arm just staying around her, not pulling, not letting go.

"You seem familiar," he finally said.

She shook her head no, and as much as she wanted to step forward and lay her head on his chest, she stepped back instead, and his arm dropped.

"Are you okay?" he asked gently.

As she looked at him, she was pretty sure he knew. The knowledge was there, in his eyes, but maybe out of respect for her grief, or respect for where they were, he didn't say anything.

"I'll be okay. It's going to take time and care before it feels right."

He nodded. "I've heard time heals. I guess I don't know. Other than seeing what's happened to other people. Although, there are some things in our lives that are just as vivid today as they were when they happened. Things that aren't like anything else. Things that feel like once-in-a-lifetime things."

She couldn't look up. She knew exactly what he was talking about. Maybe he was too considerate to come right out and say *you're the lady that I met at the beach*.

She supposed she had something she needed to tell him. But she couldn't imagine the news would be welcome. There still was no ring on his finger.

There were too many other things for her to think about right now to spend too much time thinking about that.

"Thank you for your wisdom and thank you for the words. I'm sure time will heal this." Time would also show the other thing he was talking about.

If he hugged her now, she would feel different than she had several months ago.

Would he notice?

Lifting her chin, she said, "I know I'm not walking away from him, but it feels like it."

"If it will help, I'll walk beside you."

She didn't want to be weak, but maybe there were just some times in a person's life when they needed a shoulder, and Jordan's father hadn't been that for her.

Maybe that was well and good, since she wouldn't have been a very good shoulder for him, either.

She hoped she would have been able to come together for the sake of their child.

Right now, it didn't matter that her ex wasn't here. God had given her someone else. And she wasn't going to turn his offer down. She looked up at him. "Do you mind?"

"I want to," he said.

That made her face relax into what might have been a smile on any other day but didn't quite make it to that point on this one.

He put his arm around her. "Do you mind?"

She leaned into his side. "I need it."

His hand rubbed down her arm, like it had earlier this spring, and she tried to think about that instead of about the steps she was taking away from the casket. Tried to think about the gentleness of his hands, and the softness of his lips, and the scrape of his stubble across her skin. The shadow of his head over hers, and their fingers threading together.

The thought of new life, new life for the one that had been taken.

It wasn't right, she wasn't saying it was right, but maybe instead of thinking that God was punishing her, maybe in some way it was a gift from Him.

A life for a life.

She put a hand on her stomach, then dropped it immediately, remembering that Iva May had said that's how she'd known.

"Are you okay?" he asked with concern, maybe thinking she was sick.

"Yes. Fine." She pressed against him and matched her steps to his, which she was sure were slower and smaller for her.

It was what he had done before. He gave some, and so did she, and everything had ended up in a beautiful compromise.

They stepped out of the sanctuary, and he opened the outside door, turning slightly so he could walk through without taking his hand away.

There were only three cars in the parking lot. Her mom stood beside theirs, the June sun warm, probably too warm to sit in a car.

She felt bad. She forgot her mom would be waiting.

"I hope I don't ever have to make a walk like that again," she whispered.

"I hope if you do, there's someone to walk beside you. No one should have to make a walk like that alone."

He didn't say he'd be there to walk with her, but she wondered if maybe they'd met a couple more times, if that would have been something he would have said.

Regardless, she wasn't going to make any decisions now.

"I...I hope I get to see you again," he said as they made it to the car, and he opened her door. Once her mother had seen them coming, she'd gotten in the car but left the door open, waiting.

Anitra shook her head. She didn't have space in her brain for that right now. As much as she might want it, she knew she couldn't make rational decisions in the state she was in. "I don't think I'm going to be very good company for a while."

"I know. I didn't mean right now. I meant...sometime."

She nodded.

And then, confirming that he knew who she was, he said, "You still have my card?"

She nodded again. "I never looked at it. But it's still on my refrigerator."

"Tell me you'll call me when you're ready. Please."

She turned to face him, everything that had happened, everything they'd done together between them, and her eyes on his, her feelings on her face and reflected in his, his hand on her shoulder, and hers pressing tight under her diaphragm.

"You really want me to promise?" She couldn't understand why he would.

"I do."

She nodded. "I will."

It might be years. Maybe she should warn him. She didn't feel like she would ever be ready to make a call like that, but she didn't say anything.

She needed to stop leaning on him and get in her car, but his mouth came down and brushed her forehead, and he whispered, "Please take care of yourself. If you won't let me do it for you, please."

"I can't let you. I don't...I can't...I don't trust myself."

How could she tell him that she'd made one terrible mistake? That the time that she'd spent with him had been after she'd received notice that her divorce was final, and it hadn't been something that she normally did? Probably wasn't something she would have done, if she hadn't been so upset. She wanted him to know what terrible decisions she made when she wasn't in control of herself. When her emotions were messed up.

"I don't understand, but I respect it. It's your decision." He paused, and his arm moved from her arm, to her back, and down to her waist. There wasn't much of an indent anymore in the front, but there was still a curve in her spine. His hand felt hot. "I'll be around."

She wasn't sure what he meant by that. She figured if he was working at the Blueberry Beach Hospital on a regular basis, he probably was around.

"Thank you." She meant thank you for respecting her decision, not necessarily thank you for being around, but she supposed thanks for both were in order.

It was so very nice to know that someone was beside her. Supporting her.

Of course, the business owners up and down the street had shocked her by being there for her just like that.

Just like John.

"Take care, Anitra."

It didn't occur to her until later to wonder how he knew her name.

Chapter 15

THE NEXT MORNING, JOHN was making omelets in the kitchen at the diner, but his mind was on the woman upstairs. Wondering if she'd come down. Wondering how long it would be. Not today. Tomorrow? Next week?

He would wait much longer than that. But there'd been something different about her, some kind of change he couldn't put his finger on. Although he was sure she was the woman at the beach, he couldn't believe it.

He had an idea now why she'd done what she did with him.

He, on the other hand, didn't have any such excuse, other than he felt compelled to be with her, more than anyone else, ever. He hadn't even realized there could be this attraction that wasn't just physical, but it was like his spirit longed to be with hers.

It was bad enough when they were apart. When he was holding her, it was almost impossible to resist.

And he hadn't. To his shame.

"Your head's in the clouds this morning," Iva May said as she walked into the kitchen. "That's the second omelet you've burned."

He yanked his head out of the clouds long enough to realize she was right. His nose had been telling him that for a while, although he hadn't noticed.

"You're right. Maybe I should call in sick today."

"Aren't you feeling well, John?" she asked immediately, concern oozing out of every pore of her body.

"Physically, I'm okay. Mentally, I'm a little shook up."

He hadn't been able to sleep. He'd been searching everywhere for the lake woman, and she'd been under his nose this whole time.

Not only that, but he couldn't believe he hadn't recognized her when she brought Jordan in.

Having been as intimate with her as two people could be, then to see her right in front of him and he hadn't even known it.

Maybe because he'd been so busy fighting his unprofessional feelings. Doctors couldn't have those kinds of feelings toward a patient. Or toward his patient's mother.

Belatedly, he realized she'd probably recognized him. He seemed to remember a look on her face that he hadn't understood, and he supposed that was it—recognition.

And then to have been working in her diner the whole time. Maybe unconsciously, he had recognized the lady who set his plate down, that it was really his beach lady even though he hadn't allowed himself to believe that, since his training dictated that he needed evidence in order to believe.

He could blame it on his training, but it was more likely simple stupidity on his part.

Man stupidity.

She had known it the whole time, and in hindsight, that's why she had a cap pulled down low over her eyes and hadn't looked at him.

And had disappeared and not come out the rest of the time he was there.

He understood now what hadn't been obvious at the time.

He felt like he was more observant than the average person, but obviously, he'd been completely wrong about himself.

No wonder he'd made it to his fifth decade without getting married.

But that was a good thing, because he wouldn't have wanted to be. He felt like anyone other than Anitra would have been the wrong woman.

Obviously, God had been guiding him.

Of course, he'd stepped out of the plan when he'd allowed things to go further than they should have earlier this spring.

And then a thought hit him, one that should have a long time ago, considering he was a doctor.

Of course, just because he was a doctor didn't make him wiser than the average bear.

Obviously.

She could be pregnant.

That might have been the difference that he'd sensed rather than really saw.

The reason why her waist looked thicker at the viewing.

At the funeral, she was wearing more of a flowing outfit, he remembered.

He was pretty sure that going through what she'd been through the last three months wouldn't have made her gain weight.

Unless she was nursing a new life.

"Are you just gonna stand there and stare at that griddle, or are you gonna put an omelet on it?" Bill asked. "You've got six orders sitting there."

Head in the clouds again. He hadn't gotten anything made since Iva May had interrupted him.

He took a breath, almost certain he was right, knowing he couldn't do anything about it.

He couldn't confront her, not now. Only a jerk would do it now.

And, speaking of jerks, her husband, the father of Jordan, hadn't been around as far as he knew.

"Did Jordan's dad ever make it to the viewing or funeral?" he asked Bill, who was buttering toast.

Bill glanced up at him as John poured eggs on the griddle. "No. I haven't seen the guy around for years. As far as I know, he didn't come back even when Jordan was sick."

The bowl wobbled in John's hand, and he tried to focus. It made him angry. And he had to force himself to set the bowl down carefully.

This was the first time he really had trouble focusing on making omelets. Most of the time, it didn't take too much concentration. The last few days had been a roller coaster.

He wouldn't call them emotional. He didn't really think of himself as an emotional person, but he really did have his heart and soul set on Anitra, and even though he knew he was going to have to wait, the idea that she might be carrying his child had stirred the pot even more.

The idea of her ex... Yeah. It made him jealous. Which was crazy, since she was divorced, and he wasn't even in the picture, hadn't even visited.

If John couldn't outdo that dude, he had some serious issues of his own and he definitely didn't deserve Anitra.

"You know, she's going to need some time," Bill finally said, picking up a plate and throwing two slices of bread into the toaster.

"I know." He didn't try to argue with Bill that he wasn't interested, or whatever Bill was implying, because whatever Bill was implying, he could multiply it by one hundred. By a million. He was almost at the point where he didn't care what people knew.

But he did care what Anitra thought and how she felt.

"I figured you knew it. Wasn't saying anything by it, just...I guess everyone here feels a little protective of Anitra. She's been given a hard go of it. Especially lately."

"I can see that."

"'Course, some people might say she made a bad decision. I don't know any of us who haven't."

John's head snapped up, thinking that Bill was talking about the decision she'd made on the beach early this spring.

It was a terrible decision for her, and John regretted it for that.

Beyond the guilt though, and the regret, the memories were sweet. He didn't believe in bludgeoning himself over the head with his mistakes.

He hoped Anitra didn't either.

He didn't consider it a mistake even. A misstep. A sin for sure. But a mistake? He couldn't categorize it that way.

Even though maybe he should.

He managed to make it through the morning without burning anything else, and he picked up where he'd left off at the hospital yesterday after he'd come back from the funeral.

That night, he looked through the listings that the real estate agent had sent him listlessly.

Didn't really want to pick a place out by himself.

He wanted to do it with someone.

Not just anyone.

He closed the email app without responding and went out, heading to the beach. He was a little early, and the sun wasn't down. He'd been going out and jogging or walking long enough without running into Anitra that he didn't have any ideas that he might.

It was a beautiful time of night, even if he watched alone.

Instead of heading toward the pier, like he always had before, he went in the opposite direction. The beach looked pretty much the same that way, and he walked along the edge of the waves, weaving around the people who were left after the warm sunny day.

Finally, he came to a place that was mostly deserted and went up the beach a little, not quite to the dunes, and sat down. The constant breeze that blew across the lake was warm tonight, and he lifted his face toward it.

John sat there, not bothering to read the medical journal and the latest article that he'd bookmarked for himself, and just stared at the water.

It'd been something that he'd been doing more of the last few months, and he felt like he was becoming recharged. Maybe idleness was not a bad thing.

The sky was ablaze with deep orange and pinks and lighter blues when he saw the figure coming down the beach.

He knew it was her without her having to come any closer. He recognized the billowing dress, and although the hair wasn't as long as it was in the spring, it still blew over her shoulder.

The dress pressed against her body, and from the angle he was at, he could see the slight curve of her stomach.

He was sure that what he'd suspected was true, but he wanted to ask nonetheless.

Still, he didn't move. He'd given her his number; she said she still had it. She could get a hold of him if she wanted to. For goodness' sake, he was in her diner every day.

How much more did he have to do?

How much more did she have to do to convince him that she wasn't ready to talk to him?

Maybe she never would be. So he sat still, just watching as she walked along closer.

Praying that he would have the strength to stay where he was and let her go by.

Chapter 16

FOR THE FIRST TIME in weeks, Anitra went out on the beach at sunset. It was her favorite time, followed closely by sunrise where there was a beautiful reflection and a peaceful tranquility most mornings that made it absolutely gorgeous, but the sky and the reflection on the water made sunset her favorite time.

As long as Jordan was in the house, she hadn't felt like she could leave, couldn't lose one single moment of the time she had left with him.

And now, now that he wasn't, she still didn't want to go.

She had forced herself out, but she couldn't go in the direction of the pier.

Too many memories. Her hands swung loosely at her sides, although she was tempted to put one over her stomach at that thought.

She should have told Dr. Chambers. But she couldn't. Not right after the funeral of her son. She would eventually. She had his card. And she would take it and use it at some point.

She wasn't quite sure when she first noticed the figure sitting up next to the dunes, and she wasn't sure what made her do a double-take.

She almost laughed to herself.

She knew who it was. Did he avoid the pier, too?

The idea hurt her feelings slightly, irrationally. Surely the memories weren't terrible.

Maybe they were for him. He hadn't seemed to act like they were yesterday.

She wasn't in a huge rush to get on with her life, figuring it was okay to mourn her son.

At the same time, she didn't want to get stuck in the mourning.

She had plans for tomorrow, and now, seeing John sitting a little on the rise, out in the open, where, at least for another twenty minutes or so, anyone could see him, she changed the directions of her steps and walked toward him.

"Is it okay if I sit down here?" she asked, the tone of her voice hopefully conveying as clearly as she could that if he said no, he wouldn't hurt her feelings.

She wanted to respect his privacy. He'd done such a good job of respecting hers, even though he knew who she was. Now.

"I would love it if you would," he said, and she believed him.

"Thank you." She sat beside him, sitting with her knees tucked up, feeling them push against her stomach, knowing it wouldn't be too much longer that she'd be able to do that.

He had his legs stretched out in front of him and had been leaning back on his hands, but when she sat down, he straightened, putting his hands on his lap in front of him.

"Hard to keep my eyes on the sunset when there's someone else I'd rather watch," he said, and it made her cheeks heat a little. She thought there was a compliment in there. A gentle one.

He was a gentle man, and she stopped her mind from going any further with that thought.

"You look lonely sitting here by yourself."

"Maybe that's because I am."

"That thought makes me sad."

"You have plenty to be sad about."

She bit her lip, not wanting to destroy the light tone they'd established but not ready to push her memories of her child away. "I'm trying to be happy about him. I know I should be. I just miss him. And, I guess like any parent, I had dreams of watching him grow up. His first date, his driver's license, wondering about the woman that he'd marry and the career he'd have."

"It's hard to let go of those things."

She sighed, blowing out her breath and taking another one that fortified herself. "It was a little easier, because of what you and I had done."

His head turned, and he looked at her, his brows lowered, like he was trying to figure out how the hours that they'd spent together could have alleviated anything.

And then she looked closer at his face, and she realized he knew. "I can't believe you didn't say anything."

"I didn't know right away, then I figured you'd tell me when you're ready. I hoped...I hoped you'd be ready at some point."

She nodded. "I would. I was planning on it. In fact, this seemed like a great opportunity. A wonderful opening, but you already know. How long?"

He understood right away she was asking how long he had known. "I figured it out yesterday. Took me long enough, didn't it?"

"No. It was the furthest thing from either of our minds, I'm sure."

"I can understand how it would be far from your mind, but I can't believe I lost sight of that. I guess I was...too wrapped up in you."

"Maybe we started a little backwards."

"I like that you said we started. I hope that means there is an 'us' in the future to continue."

She had hardly thought he was thinking that. She didn't know what his thoughts might be. She didn't want to make assumptions. "I hope so."

She hoped he didn't want to go too quickly though. It was nice to get out of the house and think about something other than sickness and death, even for just a few minutes, although she felt guilty somehow, but she wasn't ready to shed her mourning. Not even close.

He alleviated that fear with his next words. "I hope so too...I figured now wasn't really the time for me to say anything. That's what

I meant when I told you about the card, although..." He looked out across the lake, at the sun and the changing orange and constant movement reflected in the water. "I meant that if you need me before you want me, I'm here." His head turned toward her. "If that makes sense."

She smiled, knowing exactly what he meant. "It does."

He nodded. "Good. I hope you mean that. Because it eases my mind to know that you can get a hold of me if you need to."

"I hope to not need to. I know that I don't expect to be completely back to normal soon, whatever that is, but I want to get back into my regular routine. Maybe a week?"

He nodded. "I think everyone's different. I think that you'll find guidelines, but I think that you could probably just go by what you feel like you're ready for. Unless you find yourself staying in bed all day under the covers for weeks at a time." He turned his face and allowed his eyes to roam over her, which made her warm. "Since you're out here, I assume that's not a problem. Can I say I admire your strength?"

"It's not strength. It's just stupid stubbornness. It's as bad as it is good."

"Stubborn?" he asked, the corners of his mouth tilting.

She nodded. "It's a terrible affliction, one I've had all my life."

"If that's what's got you out here on the beach right now, I'd say it's not affliction, it's an asset."

"Well, maybe it's half-and-half, but I'm not sure the good outweighs the bad."

"I guess we all have our afflictions."

"Oh? The doctor has a weakness?"

His teeth showed a little at that, and it made her happy to make him smile. "A one-track mind. I think one thing at a time. I like to think about a problem until I solve it. Time gets away from me. I can stay at the hospital until ten or eleven o'clock at night and not even notice. Not real great for my social life."

"I suppose a wife would be annoyed at that as well."

"I don't know. I've never been married."

"Really? Is that why?"

"I guess." He looked at his hands, stretching out his fingers before seeming to deliberately relax them. "It's not that I wasn't interested in girls. Everyone always said I was too picky, or too busy, or too focused on my work, but I just never found someone that kept me from being able to concentrate on what I was supposed to, someone I wanted to think about all the time, someone who pulled me. Not just a physical attraction, but like her spirit called mine. Not..." He looked over at her. "Until you."

Her chest burned, and it felt like her blood had pins in it as it zipped up and down through her arteries, making her warm and tingly all over.

"I guess that makes me extremely blessed." It was all she could think of to say.

"I shouldn't have said anything. I'm sorry. I swore to myself that I wouldn't go after you. I've given you plenty of opportunities, figured out who you were. I figured out that you carry my child. I saw you at the viewing and the funeral..."

He almost seemed like he was about to say something else, but he didn't, and it made her wonder if there was somewhere else. She had taken a few walks on the beach, but with trying to spend every moment she could with Jordan, she hadn't been out much. Maybe he'd seen her the few times she'd been out.

"You need time," he finally said. "I can wait." His posture seemed to wilt. "No pressure, either."

She bit her lip, knowing that she was about to ask something that he might take the wrong way. She hoped she said it right.

"Would you...would you be interested in being friends, in the meantime?"

His eyes slanted to hers before he looked back out at the sunset which was fading from the peak of its glory.

She followed his gaze, watching the ripples of the lake reflect the orange and blues and pinks. Then higher, some of the brighter stars peeked out in the field of fading violet.

He seemed to be taking an awful long time to answer, and she tried not to worry her lip. She couldn't deny she was attracted to him. It was obvious.

But, honestly, she wanted more than attraction. She wanted more than someone to turn to in the night. She'd been that for someone already, and it hadn't been enough to keep him, and she'd ended up alone.

She wanted someone she could laugh with, and have fun with, and stand beside when things were hard, and hold hands with and skip beside when things were fun.

Was it so impossible to think that a marriage could be all of that?

She already knew turning to him in the night wouldn't be a problem.

Maybe it was a sigh, maybe he was just breathing out, but he took a deep breath and then said, "I want to be friends. I think, I think...what I want with you includes friendship for sure. But I wouldn't be being honest with you if I didn't say that I want more." His head turned toward her, and she could see his sincerity, even in the dim light. "I'll be friends. I want to be friends. But I need to know that we are working toward more. It doesn't have to be a fast walk, it can be a crawl. I don't care. But I don't want to be stuck being friends forever, without adding to that. Is that terrible?"

"No. That's fair. We're going into this knowing exactly what you want and exactly what I need. Which is a friend right now. And..." She had looked down, because she was talking to him like an adult, but she was still slightly embarrassed because of the things they had done together when she hadn't even known his name. Not something she'd ever done before. "I know I want more. I...have guilty feelings over the 'more' that we've already had."

He started to talk, but she put her hand up. "But those memories are beautiful, and I cherish them. It was... You were... You made me feel beautiful. Cherished. I've never felt like that before."

By the time she was done talking, she was looking at her hands on her knees, fiddling with her thumbs, and wanting to be honest, but embarrassed as well.

His hand landed beside hers on her knee, soft and light. "Thank you for saying that. I wondered if maybe, maybe it was something I had done wrong that night that made you not want to see me again. I'm... I guess you were able to figure out that it's not something I've done much."

She had gotten that impression. And now, she was wondering if he could have said "ever" instead of "much."

She doubted it, but she appreciated him confirming what she had suspected. And she was glad that she had said what she had, even though it had been hard. Obviously, he'd needed the reassurance.

Maybe, maybe sometime she could offer him more. Because he deserved it.

They sat in silence for a little longer, until the sky was black and the stars were out and the wind turned chilly rather than cool.

"Would you... Would you walk me back to my apartment?"

"As a friend?" he asked with a little tilt of his lips.

"Yes."

He stood, brushing the sand off himself, and reached a hand out for her.

She took it and stood, doing the same.

"Do friends hold hands?" he asked.

"I think they do." The answer felt easy and natural.

"Do friends go to their baby's doctor appointments with the mother-to-be?" he asked, casually, she thought, as they started up the beach.

"My friend wants to?" she asked, unused to someone who was truly interested in her...in "them," meaning her and their child.

"He does. He really wants to," he said, his eyes slanting over to hers.

She nodded. "I haven't gone to any doctors' appointments. I guess...I guess you know what my life has looked like, since I found out. I know I need to."

"I can get your prenatal vitamins."

"Wow. I hadn't thought of the perks of having a doctor for a friend."

"There are all kinds of perks. That's just the beginning." She heard the tease in his voice responding to the tease in hers.

"I'm taking over-the-counter prenatals, which are not quite the same, but close."

"I'll look into the differences tomorrow and come up with something for you." He paused. "If that's okay? As a friend."

She smiled.

"And a father. Can I be both?"

"You can, but you're starting to confuse me. I'm sure you probably read in one of your medical journals that a woman's brain cells are halved for the entirety of her pregnancy."

He looked taken aback for a moment, like he'd never heard of such a thing, before he understood and nodded sagely. "Yes. I believe it's in the introduction to every textbook as well."

She laughed, glad he was willing to play along. And suddenly she realized she'd gone for several minutes without thinking of Jordan.

The thought hit her hard and made her feel guilty. Then she realized she shouldn't feel guilty, she should be happy.

"For the last several minutes, I haven't been focused on the loss of my son."

"I see." His hand squeezed hers. "Maybe you're going to have another one." There was a little bit of uncertainty in his voice, a question, like he was wondering if that was okay.

While grief still felt heavy in her heart, there was something in her that felt lighter, too. “I hope. A little girl would be nice. Does my friend have a preference?”

“He prefers their mother to be healthy and for his child to be healthy as well.”

His words were serious, and she thought immediately of the cancer that Jordan had fought.

“I agree. More than anything.” Her words held more emotion than she wanted them to, but after losing a son to cancer, health was far, far more important than gender.

“Their mother, more than anything,” he said.

“You don’t know how many times I wished I could have taken Jordan’s cancer into my body. I would have if I could. Taken the pain, I would have taken everything.”

“Shhhh.” He touched her lips with his finger. “Stop that. If you start talking like that, I’m going to forget that I’m supposed to be a friend, and I’m going to put my arm around you, I’m going to pull you tight, and it’s going to be hard to let you go.”

“I’m sorry.”

“Don’t apologize. I think that’s the mother coming out in you, and I love it. You protect your baby with everything, and that’s a mother’s job.”

“I hope so. Because that’s right. That’s how I felt.”

“I’m sure there are differences, but...I feel that way about you.”

For some reason, his words made her want to cry. Her ex had never made her feel safe and protected. He’d never been gentle and seldom kind. Never considered it. Although, at the beginning, surely they did have some good times together. She married him for some reason, but she suspected it was mostly because he begged her and she couldn’t resist.

She should have been stronger.

They made it to her apartment, their hands still joined, and he stopped at the back door.

"Who lives there?" he asked, indicating the cottage behind them on the other side of the alley.

"Iva May. It was easy for her to run over and sit with Jordan for a bit in the evening so I could take a walk on the beach. It used to be that Jordan would go with me. Then, after he got sick, she watched him so I could go myself. It was just a little bit of time to de-stress."

"We all need that. I've actually been realizing lately how much."

"You have a hard job." She had thought about how difficult it must be to see terribly sick people and give bad news to them on an almost daily basis.

"I chose it. On purpose, because I was hoping I could do some good in the world. After so many years, I'm not sure that the answer to cancer lies in the cure but more in the prevention. At least, that's the feeling that I've been getting, and that's what my research has been telling me."

"How could I have prevented Jordan's?" The idea that she could have prevented it made the guilt expand painfully in her chest.

"I don't know." He shook his head. "Children's cancers are so much different than adults'. But there has to be something. I don't know. I'm not even sure it's something that we can prevent. Not totally."

"They said that about smallpox too, I'm sure." Relief felt cool. If John wasn't even sure there was anything she could have done, it was out of her hands.

He grinned. "All right, smarty. You could be right. I think that the Lord has a hand in it. It has to do with sin and the fall of man."

"That's interesting. So you don't have hopes of eradicating it?"

"That's a big hope. But yeah. I definitely do. Maybe it's just a challenge He's given us to try to overcome. I don't know. But I don't believe in lying down and rolling over and just letting things happen. I want to be there, doing what I can to fight and prevent. And, honestly, the more I fight, the more I feel prevention is better."

"You're kind of quiet and don't really look like a fighter."

"Not a physical fighter. It's more a war in the mind."

"I wonder if that has something to do with it?" Maybe all that positive thinking stuff was onto something.

"Maybe. I think everything is connected. The gut too. It has a lot to do with our health, even our emotional health, which contributes toward physical health. It's kind of crazy how it's all connected, but it makes sense when you think about it."

"Of course, it's all in one body. All the systems work together. It makes sense that they're not separate. We like everything to be in little compartments, but that's really not the way things work."

"That's true. A body, a world. We separate the world into countries, we speak differently and sometimes don't associate with each other at all, but everything affects everything else."

"It sounds like you're a global person."

"No," he said firmly. "I believe in fences. I won't let just anyone in my yard. There have to be boundaries. Even with our bodies...the digestive system, for example, there are boundaries to keep it separate from the circulatory system. Only certain things get through. That's just common sense. Nature."

"All right. Good points. I agree about the boundaries."

He nodded, and she figured they had said a lot without saying too much at all. She liked what she saw, and she got the feeling that maybe he did too.

"Are you gonna be okay tonight? A sincere question, as a friend."

She swallowed and tried to smile a little bit while nodding. "I'll be fine. I'll probably have some moments, but I think they are probably moments that I need to get through on my own."

"If you were married, you'd have someone to hold onto to get through those moments. Someone to share them with." He spoke casually, and she didn't feel like he was pressuring her in any way, just telling her that it was okay to need someone, since that's how they were made. "So, maybe you don't need to get through them on your own."

"You're right. I don't know that God meant for us to get through something like this alone."

"That wasn't an argument in favor of spending the night with me, that was just logic to throw out there."

"I understood that." She sighed. "Since I'm not married, I suppose it means I need to do it alone."

"I'm hoping that changes," he said, still in a way that made her not feel pressured.

"It will. Unless you change your mind."

"It's not changing," he said firmly. "That's a promise."

"Nice. I hope you're a friend who keeps his promises."

"I'm a man who keeps my word. You can count on it."

"That would be a nice change," she said sincerely. There was sadness and longing in her mind, but hopefully, it didn't color her words too much.

"As a friend, can I give you my number so you can text me when you get up to your apartment?"

"Isn't it on your card?"

"My email address is on there, and my professional number. Not my private cell phone. You can get a hold of me there, but I wanted to give you the cell phone number that my friends have."

She smiled, feeling cared for, which eased some of the sting of her loss and smoothed that over with the warmth she realized she needed.

He gave her his number, and she programmed it into her phone.

"Now, let me know when you get up, okay?"

"How about you text me when you get home? It'll take you longer."

"I'm not going to turn that down." He hesitated for just a second. "Good night."

"Good night."

He squeezed her hand and then let go as she opened her door and slipped in.

Chapter 17

ORIGINALLY, ANITRA had intended to go down the next morning and talk to everyone who had been helping in her shop.

She owed them more than she could say. Because of them, it hadn't mattered that her ex had stolen the money out of their account. She'd had enough to live on, because of the daily deposits they'd made sure had gotten in the bank.

But between the low of the funeral and Jordan's death and her eyes landing on something that belonged to him, or her brain recalling something they'd done together, or a memory that came in, and the high from being with John and the memories he brought to mind, she felt like she was riding a tossing ship on the ocean.

Crying one moment and sighing the next.

The highs and lows were probably exaggerated, feeding off each other. Whatever it was, she was a mess.

She never went down.

After lunch, a long crying spell, and then a nap, she did walk over to Iva May's cottage and knock on the door.

"Come in. It's open," Iva May called, her voice coming clearly through the open windows.

"Oh my goodness, girl. I didn't expect to see you. Is everything okay?" Iva May got up, setting her knitting aside and walking over to Anitra, concern replacing the surprise on her face.

"I'm fine. Mostly. I guess I just wanted to talk to someone, and you know everything."

"My goodness, that's a heavy burden for me to bear," Iva May said with a little twinkle in her eyes, her face still pinched.

"No. Nothing terrible. I just... I need to thank everyone for what they've done for me. But at the same time, I know I need to announce this pregnancy."

"I know, honey. That's going to be hard, because you're afraid of peoples' reactions. Come on in and sit down. I'll get some tea."

"Thanks." Anitra walked in, and as Iva May put the kettle on to boil, she went to the cupboard and got two cups out, feeling almost as at home at Iva May's cottage as she did at her mother's or her own place.

"You don't have to be in any rush to tell anyone," Iva May said as she opened the refrigerator and got the cream out.

"I'm showing. John... I guess I didn't tell you about John."

"And you don't have to."

"I need to. He's the father. Of course. He guessed last night." She straightened the cup so that both handles were parallel to the counter. "Actually, I guess he figured it out at the funeral. I hadn't told him and had barely seen him."

"Well, you do have that tell I told you about. I suppose someone who knew you as well as he did—"

"That's just it. He doesn't know me at all."

"He... He must've known you fairly well," Iva May said, letting her sentence dangle.

Anitra's cheeks heated, and she was tempted to put her hands on them. "Of course. Of course he did."

Goodness. She'd been married. She had a child. This shouldn't be something she had a problem talking about.

"It's natural that he would notice. Other people don't know you that well."

"That's true. Thank you. I hadn't thought of that. Stupidly, I hadn't thought of that."

"Don't beat yourself up. You just lost a child. You're not supposed to be thinking straight. You're supposed to need us. And the people who are helping you in the diner do understand that."

"Do they? I feel like they've given me more than I can ever repay. I feel like I need to go back immediately."

"I can tell them tomorrow that I told you to stay away for another week. Don't set foot in the kitchen. Don't set foot in the diner. Just go, sit on the sand, look at the lake, and let your soul heal."

The idea felt heavenly. The idea that she didn't have to face everyone right away and she had a little time to get herself together. To get used to not having Jordan to take care of.

To get used to the idea of falling in love, which was really odd to think about next to the death of her child.

But it was beautiful in a way too. Having the new child growing within her, feeling the highs and the warmth and the sweet smiles and secret thoughts of falling in love balancing out the lows.

Not everything with Jordan was low. She had that picture of him playing baseball in heaven. That was a definite high.

Her phone chimed with a text. She couldn't stop the smile that lifted her lips as she saw it was from John.

"That must be good news," Iva May said as the teakettle started to whistle.

Anitra nodded as she set the sugar container on the table beside the cream. "It's from John."

She tapped on it and read the message on her screen.

I hope it's okay... I talked to the OB/GYN here at Blueberry Beach and asked if they would make an appointment and call you with the date and time? I'll call right back if that was your friend overstepping.

Iva May had busied herself wiping the counter, so Anitra texted back.

It needed to be done. Thank you. I'll watch for their call.

Thanks for not getting upset. I should have asked last night.

I assume you did it because you care about your friend. Why would that upset me?

Because maybe I'm taking control and overstepping.

I didn't think that way at all. But if it was, it was because you cared. Also, you're the father. It makes me happy that you care about your baby.

I'm glad. Because I do. About both of you.

She sighed, putting her phone away but relishing the warm feeling that he gave her in her chest. So much different than her ex.

Who hadn't even cared to come to his son's funeral.

She could understand how a funeral was hard. She, herself, didn't want to go in some ways. But... He hadn't even visited.

"Everything all right?" Iva May asked.

"It was. John is having the obstetrician call me and set up an appointment."

"Wow. He's...having them call you?" Iva May said, and Anitra realized how weird that was.

"He's a doctor. This must be a perk of having a doctor as the father of my child."

"Nice perk," Iva May said in a tone that held admiration. " I'm sure there are others."

Anitra thought of the prenatals John had talked about. He hadn't mentioned those in his text.

She smiled anyway. "I guess you're probably right."

She fiddled with her phone before shoving it back in her pocket. "Can we talk about normal things? Can you tell me what's been going on? What I've missed?"

"Oh, you know there's always something going on," Iva May said as she poured the tea into the teacups, holding the teabags' strings so they didn't go in the cup.

"I know. I know I've missed stuff. How's Gage doing? Has he found someone?" Anitra asked, mentioning the single dad who lived with his daughters across the street above the candy and ice cream shop.

"My goodness, girl, you haven't been gone that long. That man moves slower than a sleeping turtle."

"Well, I can always hope."

"Keep hoping, girl, because nope. He's just as single as he's always been. His poor daughters would really like to have a mother. Well. Maybe they wouldn't like one. But they need one." Iva May set the teacup down in front of Anitra and then pulled a chair out and settled herself in it with her own teacup. "But let me tell you, I'm actually holding out some high hopes for Bill."

Anitra listened as Iva May filled her in on everything that had been going on.

By the time she left an hour later, her spirits had been lifted and her heart unburdened.

She felt comfortable waiting a week, just taking it for herself.

Then she'd get started on seeing what she could do to pay everyone back.

She'd just gotten into her apartment and was thinking about taking a shower when her phone rang.

She didn't recognize the number, but the name had OB/GYN after it, so she assumed this was from John's friends.

"Hello?"

"Hello. May I speak to Anitra Pollard, please?"

"This is she," Anitra said, her stomach turning a little. She needed to make this appointment, and she didn't need to be nervous about it.

"I'm calling because Dr. Chambers requested that you be given an appointment as soon as possible. When would suit you?"

What day suited her? Was she just supposed to pick a day?

"Um, you have openings?"

"For Dr. Chambers, we make them."

Oh.

"Tomorrow?"

She supposed since John had taken the trouble to do this for her, she should do it as soon as she could.

"Morning or afternoon?" the receptionist asked.

"Either is fine."

"How about tomorrow morning at ten o'clock?"

"That's perfect."

The receptionist gave her instructions to get to the right building on the hospital campus, and the call ended.

She set her phone down and then thought about texting John.

She picked it back up.

Your OB/GYN called, and I made an appointment for tomorrow at ten o'clock.

He responded immediately. **Wonderful. Thank you. Am I still allowed to go?**

Of course. Please.

She'd always wanted her husband to go, and he'd never made time.

As a father? Or as a friend?

Both?

Thank you. Happily. I'm sorry I'm excited. This is my first time.

This isn't my first time. And I'm still excited.

I'm going to need to stay late tonight, in order to be able to get off tomorrow. I won't be on the beach.

Thank you for letting me know. I think I'll take a walk anyway.

It seems to be safe. But I'd appreciate it if you'd be careful.

Of course.

I guess...I guess you wouldn't consider not going?

No. An evening walk on the beach is something I've done all my life.

I know. I'm sorry.

Thank you for not being upset.

Her ex would have been unhappy if he'd told her he didn't want her to do something and she'd done it anyway. Of course, John didn't exactly say no. Didn't exactly command her not to do something, and he didn't seem upset.

I know you'll probably be fine. I just...worry.

Don't.

I'll try to listen to the lady.

Thank you. It was a friendly suggestion.

I'll remember that. Text me when you get back in?

Of course.

It warmed her heart that he wanted her to.

She set her phone down and went to take a shower, smiling, even when she saw Jordan's shampoo sitting on the rim of the tub.

She didn't love him less, even if she started to hurt less that he was gone.

It almost felt like her love was measured in the amount of pain she had, and she had to remind herself that her love wasn't contingent on the depth of the pain she felt.

Chapter 18

JOHN STOOD IN FRONT of the OB/GYN building, fingering his phone.

It was 9:45, and he'd been standing there for ten minutes.

They hadn't made solid plans to meet outside the building, and he could text her and let her know where he was, but he thought she might be driving, and he didn't want her to feel like she had to answer him while she was.

So, he paced back and forth.

He'd left his white coat on the hook in his office. He didn't always wear it anyway, although the pockets were handy for putting things in, and he appreciated it for that.

Not necessarily for the fact that it said he was a doctor.

He wasn't coming to this appointment with his doctor persona.

Checking his phone—one minute had gone by—he figured he'd give her until ten o'clock, and if he didn't see her, he'd text.

Maybe he should have texted earlier.

It wasn't like him to waffle on whether he should or shouldn't do something.

He stopped, laughing at himself.

Obviously, he was a first-time father and feeling the nerves.

The nerves of wanting to be a good father, the nerves of wanting the mother to want him.

He reminded himself though, how many times he'd seen men change in the first stages of a relationship, only to go back to their former selves after they caught what they were chasing.

He didn't want to be that. He didn't want to pretend to be something he wasn't, just to impress her.

It was hard not to want to put his best foot forward though.

A car pulled into the parking lot, and he perked up. It was the same silver SUV that he helped her into in the church parking lot.

It was kind of nondescript, so he watched it as it found a spot and parked.

As soon as the brown head appeared beside it, he started walking toward her.

Maybe he should wait on the sidewalk, but he supposed it didn't hurt for her to know that he was eager.

Maybe she wouldn't like it, but there it was.

"Oh my goodness. I'm glad you're here. I wasn't sure whether we were to meet here or somewhere else, but I didn't want to text while I was driving." She spoke as she got out of her car, closing the door behind her.

She wore a fairly loose shirt, although it didn't look specially made for a pregnant woman to him, and a knee-length skirt.

With sandals.

"I didn't text you for the same reason. I didn't want you to take your attention off the road."

"Well, that explains that," she said with a smile. "I wasn't sure if you'd gotten busy and maybe weren't going to make it."

He looked at his watch. "I've been standing here for twenty-five minutes. Not too busy."

"I'm sorry. I should have texted you."

"No. Don't apologize. I wanted to. Actually, I was too nervous to really concentrate on much."

"Nervous?"

"This is my first time, remember?"

"Oh. That's right. Well, I'm probably going to be in a little bit of trouble. I should have made an appointment a couple months ago."

"No." He closed her car door and took her hand as they started through the parking lot. He felt a little sheepish, and he admitted, "I already spoke to the obstetrician, Dr. Morgan. She knows that you're pregnant and how long you've been pregnant, and she knows about Jordan."

He skidded his eyes toward her to make sure that his comments weren't upsetting her.

"Okay." She looked at him under her lashes. "You know. I can do this for myself."

"I know. I keep reminding myself of that, but I am...an overachiever. I can try to back off."

"Actually, I suppose this could be a sign of someone who might end up being controlling." She gave him a glance, and he looked down. He knew he would have trouble with that. He didn't get to where he was in life by letting other people walk all over him.

She shrugged. "But it's such a refreshing change. I don't want to keep speaking poorly of my ex, but he never went to any of my appointments. I always wanted to have a partner. Isn't that the reason there's two?"

"I think I heard you say that you like me taking care of you?"

"That's right. I do. As long as you don't mind when I push back a little, if I need to."

"Like you did last night, when you told me that you were going to take a walk on the beach even though I didn't want you to."

"Right." She bit her lip. "That would have made my ex mad."

"It didn't make me mad. It made me realize I was trying to dictate what an adult could do with her free time. It wasn't my place."

"Well, it's not that it wasn't your place. I understood that you were doing it because you cared about me. But I liked that you didn't insist and you didn't get angry."

"And I like that you didn't get upset with me for everything that I did today regarding this appointment."

"No. I loved it."

"I like seeing you smile. I think I've seen you smile more now than I have the entire time I've known you." He opened the door and held it, and she walked in.

He didn't say *except the night we spent on the beach*. Because, while he thought she was smiling a lot that night, he hadn't exactly seen it.

They went in, and the receptionist gave them an iPad on which to fill out forms.

She bit her lip as she filled it out, and he wasn't sure whether that was her normal expression as she filled out paperwork, or whether she was worried about something.

Finally, he couldn't take it any longer, and he leaned over. "Is there something wrong?"

"Not really."

"So 'not really' means yes?"

She huffed out a breath that sounded like a laugh. "I guess." She sighed. "I...I forgot about insurance. After the divorce, Jordan was able to stay on my husband's policy. Of course I couldn't. I...don't have any."

He could think of an immediate solution to that problem. It was as simple as getting a license and saying vows, and then she would be covered, totally and completely.

But that wasn't the solution she needed.

"I guess this is probably where the father of the baby needs to step up and pull his share. After all, you're growing her, I should pay for her."

He said it in a way intended to make her laugh, and it worked.

"You have a beautiful laugh," he said.

That made her laugh again. "No one has ever said that I have a beautiful laugh. That's crazy."

"Well, I'm sure there are plenty of people who wanted to say it but just didn't," he said, eliciting another laugh.

"Seriously, I can't let you pay. That's not right. That's not why you're here."

"I know. I do think I suggested a fair trade. Since I can't grow the baby."

"That's true. You can't." She looked at him, then her lips turned up.

"I believe I recognize that as a superior look you're giving me, since you can do something that I can't."

"Never."

"That's okay, because I'm secure in my manhood, and I can handle it."

"Glad to hear that you're not jealous of me because I have a uterus and you don't. It might make me slightly concerned to hear that."

"I'm happy that you're happy that I'm happy I don't have a uterus."

"Dr. Chambers?"

Chapter 19

ANITRA MADE A MENTAL note to herself to tell John that he was adorable when he blushed.

He cleared his throat.

"Yes?" he said in a much more scholarly tone than he had said his last sentence.

Anitra snorted.

He shot her a glance, one that held humor and also a little private conversation. She loved it, and she smirked at him.

"I'm Dr. Morgan. I spoke with you, but I don't believe we've ever met."

He stood, taking her hand and shaking it.

Anitra stood too, liking Dr. Morgan already because of the humor that she had in her eyes. She seemed to find it funny that they had been sitting in the waiting room goofing off.

"And you must be Anitra. I've been looking forward to meeting you. Dr. Chambers is well known for his work in Chicago. I know several people who have been under his care and have had nothing but glowing reports of him. I'm eager to get to know you, and I'm honored that I've been entrusted with the care of your baby."

Anitra wasn't sure what to say. This was certainly a little different reception than she had with her first baby.

Her eyes skittered to John, and she lifted her brows.

"I don't think we're quite finished filling out forms. We were stumbling a little over the insurance. I was insisting that I wanted to pay. She was giving me a little bit of a hard time about it." He lifted his brows as though to say, *she wanted me to answer, so I'm giving my side of the story.*

Anitra rolled her eyes. When finished, Dr. Morgan was looking at her, a grin lifting both sides of her mouth.

"I see. Well, it's been five minutes, and already you guys are my most interesting case in years. How about you follow me? We'll get you to an exam room, and the nurse will take some basic information." Dr. Morgan turned her back and started walking.

John bowed a little and twirled his hand, holding it out and saying, "After you, my friend."

She snorted. "This is a really interesting time for your goofy side to come out."

"I didn't even realize I had a goofy side. If it's surprising you, think how shocked I must be."

She pursed her lips and batted her eyes. "I like it."

"I'll have to feed it, then."

"I'll help you."

"Thank you. I think you're going to be good for me."

"You've already been good for me."

She wasn't even leaving him, she was just walking ahead of him, but she didn't want to go.

Kinda crazy how that worked. She shook her head at herself, for acting like a kid when she was an adult, then she turned and followed Dr. Morgan down the hall. She was still baffled or maybe befuddled by John's turn toward the goofy. Normally, he was so serious.

Not that she minded. She liked him. A lot. Goofy and serious.

And she wondered if the goofiness was really just because he wanted to hear her laugh.

Probably if they spent time together, he would get over that.

The nurse took her blood pressure and some measurements and did all of the other things that were normal for a visit, then Dr. Morgan came in and John stepped out for a bit.

To her surprise, once Dr. Morgan had done the expected things, she announced that they would do a sonogram right in the room.

That was new since she had Jordan.

Maybe it was because of John. He seemed excited about it, although it was too early to tell whether they were having a boy or girl.

Still, the tech wheeled a portable machine in, and John stared at the screen and even asked several times for the tech to go back and redo a certain area.

She'd seen enough ultrasounds that she could kind of pick out a foot and fingers and definitely the heartbeat, which was music to her ears.

But John seemed to be able to see a little more, and while the tech took her measurements, he didn't take his eyes off the screen.

When the tech left, Anitra was confident her baby was healthy.

Their baby.

John looked a little abashed. "I hope I didn't embarrass you."

"Of course not. What made you think that?"

"Well, I suppose you're not used to having someone dictate to the tech. I just wanted to make sure that everything I saw looked right." He grinned a little. "That's the father of the baby coming out, not your friend."

"I assumed so. And I like it. And you're right. I'm not used to having someone with me. I always did this alone."

She didn't say anything more. That was over and done with. She didn't need to badmouth Danny, although it would be hard for her to come up with anything good to say.

Dr. Morgan came in after a bit. "I think everything looks good. Our dates line up, and the baby's measurements are right on schedule." She talked about scheduling the next appointment, and then as they were standing up and getting ready to go, she said to John, "I heard you're moonlighting with a second job?"

She seemed to think it was funny, and as Anitra looked between her and John and then back to her, she thought John looked a little embarrassed, and maybe he shook his head.

Dr. Morgan murmured, "Oh," and she looked at Anitra before she said, "We've been having such wonderful weather. I'm originally from the Upper Peninsula." She widened her eyes and tilted her head. "Are you from around here?"

"Yes. I grew up in Blueberry Beach, and I've lived there my whole life. It's a great town."

"It sure is. Pretty. And small enough to give you that hometown feel but large enough that you can find a nice place to eat. I love the diner there."

"That's mine," Anitra said, smiling and a little proud of herself.

"I love it! We go there quite often. At least once a month." Dr. Morgan seemed to truly be excited about it. "My children always find something good to eat, and yet there are adult things on the menu too. Plus, it's so close to the beach we always end up walking. Well, not in the winter. More likely, we'd be shoveling snow."

"True. We do get a good bit of lake effect. But I like that too."

"Snow is fun, but it's not good for business."

"Not mine. Probably it is for yours."

Dr. Morgan laughed at that, and John grunted out a surprised laugh as well.

John said, "My eyes have been opened in more than one way today."

"Now you know what to do on a cold winter night." Dr. Morgan winked.

"I think I would have thought of that myself, but thanks," John said, and Dr. Morgan exchanged a look with Anitra.

They gathered their things, and Anitra set up an appointment on the way out while John paid.

He held her hand as they walked out of the building and toward her car. "Thanks so much for letting me do that with you. I know you probably don't usually hear this, but I really enjoyed it."

"I felt better that you were there. I know you know things I don't, and it really reassures my mind to have you beside me."

"Well, don't be reassured too much. That's not the first time I've seen a sonogram, but it is the first time since residency. Still, I had fun and not just because of the medical angle." He gave her a speaking look.

"I did too. And definitely not because of the medical angle. It was because of you. Thank you."

He smiled at her compliment as he opened her car door and she got in. "I'll probably be working late again tonight. Just wanted to let you know. If you go out on the beach, will you text me?"

He didn't command her. It was most definitely a question and spoken humbly.

How could she say no to that? Not that she wanted to.

"Of course."

"Thank you. Maybe tomorrow night, we'll do it together?"

"If you're there, I will be too."

He smiled. "Drive carefully."

"Enjoy the rest of your day."

He closed her door but didn't walk away until she had backed out and started leaving. In her rearview mirror, she saw him standing there, watching her. There was something really nice about the attention and care and concern that he showed.

She soaked it all up like parched earth soaked up the soothing rain. That's how it felt. Good and perfect and right.

Chapter 20

JOHN HELD ANITRA'S hand as they walked along the beach two nights later.

She'd just told him how she'd visited Jordan's grave and planted flowers even though there was no headstone yet.

Her voice had been steady and level, and he felt like she was handling things nicely.

When he first found out about the baby he was worried about the difficulty she was going through, the death of her child, which was enough to devastate anyone, and he was concerned that perhaps it would affect her pregnancy.

He determined he would do everything he could to help her, but he also had determined he wouldn't push in.

He knew he could be pushy.

They'd lapsed into silence and strolled along at a leisurely pace as the sun sank lower on the horizon.

"Do you ever keep your diner open in the evening?" he asked, noting all the people that were still on the beach as they pushed into summer and figuring that there was a business opportunity there for her.

"No. Maybe for a very special occasion, once or twice."

"That would probably require a whole revamping of your menu and kitchen?"

"Menu, yes. Also, it would require me putting in a lot more hours. And while the extra money would be nice, and I do think I would make profit, and honestly, the thought has crossed my mind, it just never seemed worth it to give up the time that I had with Jordan. The money that I make is enough to pay the bills. We'll never be rich but... *I'll* never be rich."

Her voice sounded sad, like she'd realized that she was talking about Jordan and he wasn't there anymore.

"There will be a wee one soon," he reminded her gently.

"That's right. You know I waver back and forth as to whether God took Jordan to punish me for my sin, or whether God provided this baby to comfort me after Jordan's death. I'm not sure what to believe."

"I'm not trying to minimize the sin. God is holy, and I think sometimes in our modern day, we forget that. We want everything to be okay. Nothing off limits and we can do whatever we want. That doesn't make sense, because nothing in nature teaches us that you can do anything you want with no consequences."

He drew himself in. He could go on and on with that subject, but he didn't.

Instead, after a few more quiet steps together, he said, "We like to focus on God's love and forgiveness. He does forgive. And he does love, and I think that as long as there is repentance for the sin, it's best to focus on the fact that God wants to give you good things. A baby is a very good thing."

They had left their shoes back at the walkway when they came on the beach, and she kicked her toe in the sand.

He wasn't used to walking without shoes and had to admit he liked the feel of the sand, the texture and the temperature, under his feet.

"That's such a different attitude than most people. Danny didn't want children. He saw them as a pain. Something that kept him from getting everything he wanted."

John had to be honest. "Maybe when I was younger, I had that attitude too. I never really thought that, but I might have. I can't necessarily judge him, although I hope I wouldn't have thought that way." He took a couple more steps and figured he shouldn't hide anything. "Now, maybe I'm older. Maybe more mature. Maybe I've done the things I wanted to do and realized that there's more to life than just me and what I want. I don't know. Maybe I'm just in denial about how much work a baby takes."

She snorted at that, and he figured he probably had no clue. He sure hoped he got the chance to find out.

"I'm looking forward to it. Definitely. I can't wait. And if having a baby means I don't get everything I'm used to getting, right now, anyway, I'm excited about it."

"Well, you probably don't have any idea of what you're getting into."

"It's us, right? What we're getting into?"

"Even when I was married, I didn't feel like it was me and a partner. It felt like me doing everything myself. I might have trouble adjusting."

"Well. I have that tendency to be pushy that I already told you about. I guess I'll just keep pushing it until you let me in."

"I hope so. The idea of having someone to share this with is a really nice one."

"I've already admitted that I'm pushy, you can let me know if I'm pushing too hard."

The wind blew her dress, a strong gust, outlining her front and the curve of her stomach. It was so obvious. He couldn't have missed it. Except, he supposed, if he hadn't known what her stomach had looked like before, maybe he wouldn't have thought of it. It was all speculation now.

"I will. I suppose we're bound to disagree over some things. Things you feel strongly about that I do too. I hope we can work through those."

"I hope so too. I think we can. I suppose it will involve one of us giving in. And I don't mind doing that, as long as it's not me every time. I suppose that would get old."

"It does."

He hated that she knew that. He hated that someone had treated her like that. That someone had taken advantage of her and taken her for granted.

He hoped he didn't. But he also knew it was human nature to strive for something, and then once whatever it was that had been such a longing and a goal was in one's possession, one had a tendency to forget about it as one went on to move one's attention to other things.

"I know we agreed to be friends. And I know that it's going to take a while, and we didn't really put an end date on it. I was wondering if we could maybe revisit the idea of being more at the end of summer?"

She was quiet for a while, and he appreciated the fact that she was thinking about it and not just giving him an answer off the cuff. Tugging on her hand, he stopped her and turned her toward the sunset which had exploded across the sky. Tugging a little more, he pulled her in front of him, encouraged when she didn't resist.

He stood behind her, his feet outside of hers, his hands on her hips, then sliding around the bottom of the little bump of her stomach.

She relaxed against him, leaning her head back against his chest.

He lowered his head to her ear and whispered, "I feel like I'm holding our baby like this. Thank you for letting me."

"I feel like you're helping me carry him when you have your hands like that. Thank you."

The never-ending lake breeze blew her hair across his face, and it tickled his nose.

"That actually feels good. Your hair, I mean."

"It's annoying at times too."

"Like when you try to talk and it gets in your mouth," he said, with a hair in his mouth.

He didn't want to take his hand away from her stomach and from their baby to remove it though, so he just kept there.

"I'm feeling really well. And even though I miss Jordan, it's not a soul-tearing grief that I feel I'll never get out of. Maybe I was able to mourn some knowing for a long time that he was going to die. Or maybe..."

He tried not to hold his breath while he waited for what she was going to say.

"Or maybe it's you. I don't feel alone anymore."

"I hope I mean more to you than just a body to be beside you." That was a huge statement for him. Something he hoped with all his heart.

"Oh, you're absolutely more than a body. Everything you do makes me wonder how I managed without you."

"I like that. I think maybe that's the way it's supposed to be, if two become one. It shouldn't be a matter of two separate beings doing their own thing and going their own way, if you're truly one."

"That's a good point. One I don't typically think about."

"Maybe that's another reason to have someone else. To help you with the thoughts you don't think yourself. Two different opinions, although sometimes it's hard, a lot of times it's good."

"I agree. And not just for the different opinions, for the shoulder to lean on. Like I needed yours for the past week."

"It's here for you anytime."

She laughed a little. "What I was trying to say is I think I'm ready to go back to working and managing the diner. Iva May assured me that it was being taken care of, and I wanted to go down and thank everyone for everything they've done last week, but I knew I wouldn't be able to hold it together even to get the words out. I'll probably still cry, because I'm so overwhelmed at what my friends and neighbors have done for me, but I feel ready."

John stood in silence, waging war with himself. Should he tell her he was a part of that? If she came down to talk to everyone, she would see him.

She might think it was a betrayal that he hadn't told her right now, when he had the opportunity.

But it felt like he might be bragging, or tooting his own horn, or trying to get brownie points, or some other thing, and every way he tried to think to form the words, he just felt like he was pushing himself on her.

Maybe there was a way. But in the end, he decided not to say anything.

Chapter 21

ANITRA WOKE UP EARLY the next morning—around four AM—and couldn't get back to sleep. She kept thinking about what she could say to her friends who had helped her. Words just didn't seem to be adequate for the sacrifice they'd made for her.

Her mother, too. She supposed as a mother she would make any sacrifice necessary for her child. So while she would thank her mother, of course, and didn't expect her to have done everything she did and for no return payment, it was just a little different than having a random friend or business owner who happened to be her neighbor make such a huge sacrifice. One she would think only family and very close friends would make.

The words tumbled over and over in her head, and she finally decided to take a walk on the beach before she came in to talk to them. Maybe that would settle her jumbled mind.

She could picture herself crying and just saying *thank you, thank you, thank you* over and over.

What else could she do?

She didn't have any material goods. She couldn't pay them what they deserved. She couldn't even reciprocate, because running the diner took all of her time.

As she wrestled with that, walking slowly and lifting her face to the wind, she thought about how little gratitude she gave for the sacrifice of Christ, which was much bigger than that of her friends.

Yet she'd never walked on the beach, wrestling with herself, wondering what she could do in return.

It was just always kind of a *yeah, thanks for that* and move on.

Someone had died for her, and she treated it with less contemplation than she did her friends who had only given two months of their lives, and that in bits and pieces. Not to downplay that sacrifice, but she realized maybe her priorities were a little mixed up.

She wasn't exactly sure what she could do to be better. One didn't offer God a token candy bar in exchange for what He'd done.

She couldn't pay for it, but she could show gratitude...daily.

That was the only thing she really had settled in her mind as she walked down the path that led to the street where the Blueberry Café sat.

It was past 5 o'clock, and it was open serving breakfast, so she went in the front door.

Immediately, she saw people she recognized, and some that looked familiar, although she didn't know their names.

She stopped to chat with first one table and then another, and half an hour had slipped by, and she hadn't even realized.

She happened to be walking away from a table when the bell jingled, and a man walked in.

Her reaction was immediate and automatic. She stopped and put a hand on her stomach.

Immediately, she dropped it. She didn't want him to know.

What was Danny doing here?

He looked around the place, cocky as usual, with a bit of a smirk, until his eyes landed on her.

She hadn't gathered herself together, or he wouldn't have caught her staring.

But as his face brightened, and his chin lifted, and he started toward her, she assumed she must be the reason he was there.

The whole point for her being here this morning was to thank the people who had helped her. Not subject them to an ugly confrontation in the diner.

Not that she was planning on having an ugly confrontation, but she couldn't imagine Danny coming for anything less.

Anger roiled in her at the money he'd taken and the fact that Jordan had died without seeing his father again, feeling unloved and unwanted.

She wanted to scratch his eyes out, spit on him, hurt him somehow, the way he'd hurt their son, and anything that hurt her son hurt her as well.

All the old feelings, the ones she had when he left, had been pushed under the rug, or maybe she'd gotten over them. She didn't really care how he treated her. But it hurt her deeply that he treated their son so poorly and that Jordan had cried because of his dad.

She was standing maybe twenty feet from the door, and he was halfway to her, before she turned on her toes and walked with purpose, staring straight ahead, toward the kitchen door.

If she was going to talk to him, she wasn't going to do it here.

"Anitra. Baby. Come back."

The endearment rankled. Not because she minded being called "baby" necessarily, but because it came from him. He didn't have the right to use an endearment with her.

She ignored him. Of course.

Feeling Iva May's eyes on her as she stood at the cash register checking out a customer made Anitra want to lift her head and tell her that she would be fine.

She *would* be fine, but she didn't need to stop to say it.

She also noticed Bill, who had been delivering plates to a table, moved immediately to follow her.

Adam and Lindy, who had been sitting at the bar along the counter, stood up. Adam touched Lindy's arm, but Lindy shook her head and followed her husband.

Funny how one tuned in to the slightest detail when one was mad enough to rip someone's skin off their face.

She hoped she wasn't capable of that kind of violence, but the way she felt now, she definitely was.

Why would he show up at this point in time? Jordan was gone. There was no reason to come now. She definitely didn't want to see him.

She stormed into the kitchen, anger and frustration and hurt and pain and everything that she didn't want to feel toward her ex boiling in her stomach, narrowing her vision.

And then all she saw when she walked through the kitchen door was the man standing at the griddle.

He was flipping an omelet. She distinctly saw the mushrooms and the spinach.

Maybe she was so angry she was hallucinating. She blinked her eyes several times. But the picture didn't change. Only now, the man set the omelet back down and looked up. Probably wondering why someone had burst into the kitchen only to stop short.

"John?" she said, her voice sounding odd, her head tilted.

Questions of a different sort tumbled through her head, but she couldn't articulate any.

The frustration and the anger were still there, but she was looking at a man who was supposed to be a doctor. He was supposed to work in a hospital. He'd walked on the beach with her last night, held her baby, gave her a shoulder, and he'd never mentioned that he was going to be in her diner in the morning?

He wore an apron, and a chef's hat sat at cocky angle on his head, like someone had set it there as a joke.

In a flash, she could tell he was comfortable where he was. This wasn't his first day. He wasn't wondering what he was supposed to do. He felt at home.

The door burst open behind her. Her questions about John would have to wait. She whirled, meeting the angry eyes of her ex.

"What makes you think you're so high and mighty you can just walk away and ignore me? That's ignorant. You have no call to be so ignorant."

"I figured you'd be saying something like that to me, and I didn't want my patrons to hear it," she said, her voice now calm and articulate, despite the riot in her chest.

"When I talk to you, you acknowledge me. You don't treat me like a piece of crap and walk away from me."

"I'm listening now," she said, raising a brow and resisting the urge to cross her arms over her chest. She felt like she needed that protection.

But the kitchen door opened, and Adam and Lindy and Bill and Iva May walked through, letting the door swing shut and lining up behind her ex.

She wasn't alone. She could handle this.

Normally, her ex was a jerk but not violent.

Although he did have a hair-trigger temper, which obviously she'd triggered now by not confronting him in the diner and choosing the kitchen instead.

It was always hard to tell what was going to set him off.

"I want to talk to you. In private," he said as he came closer and took her arm, not in a terribly hard grip but firm enough to let her know he was going to ensure that she followed him. He started toward the door.

"I don't want to go with you," she said, pulling on her arm and only moving her feet as she had to to keep her balance.

"We need to talk. And we need to talk in private," Danny insisted, looking around the kitchen. "I don't know what you guys are all staring at. Go back to work."

"If you want to talk about the money you stole from my account that my lawyer is trying to get back, we don't need to go outside about that."

"Shut up."

"If you want to talk about your son, he's dead. It's too late for you to see him and too late for you to go to the funeral. I left you messages."

"We'll finish this outside, woman."

She wanted to say, *oh, I'm not baby anymore?* But she didn't. Being a smart aleck with him would only make him angrier.

"These people are my friends. Whatever you say, they're going to hear about anyway. You might as well say it in front of them."

"I believe the lady said she didn't want to leave with you." John spoke softly from where he'd stridden and stopped in front of them.

Anitra had never seen him move fast. He talked about jogging in the morning, but she'd never seen him.

He always walked with confidence, of course, but deliberately. Never hurried. Even when he was nervous in front of the OB/GYN office, his movements hadn't been jerky or fast.

How he managed to get right in front of them, she wasn't sure, since he was behind the griddle and they were going down the side of the kitchen.

But she appreciated it.

"I heard her say that, too," Bill said, coming up and standing beside John.

"The lady said it clearly. Because I heard it as well," Adam said from behind them.

Danny jerked his head around, then looked back at John and Bill standing in front of them.

She felt the anger and frustration almost radiating off her ex as he realized the odds were stacked against him.

He knew she probably wouldn't call the police, not unless he hit her, which he'd never done. But he got away with rough handling her like this and demanding his way, and she'd given in to him to keep the peace.

She knew that type of behavior was not something she should accept, but it felt better to live with it and put up with it than to fight about it. Even right now, she probably would have gone with him.

Calling the police would get her out of it, but she didn't want that kind of attention brought to the diner, not with the morning rush just getting started. Plus, he wasn't doing anything technically illegal.

She didn't want the embarrassment of being in a domestic dispute with her ex-husband. She just wanted to be left alone.

She didn't even care if she got her money back. Now that Jordan was gone, she didn't care if she ever saw Danny again. It was too late for him to do anything for Jordan, and he couldn't make that up.

"All right, that's fine." He looked down at her. His frustration was clear in the way his hand gripped her arm, but his face was set in calm lines. "If you want to talk about this in front of everyone, we can." He smiled, a charming smile. One that showed even, straight white teeth, and a square jaw, and a face that a person could expect to see on a movie screen.

He was devastatingly handsome.

He was also a jerk.

"Now, sweetie, I know that I haven't been around, and if you want me to, I can tell you what I've been doing. It's been very serious, and I just wasn't able to get away." His voice was soft and kind. It wasn't the voice of a bad person. He let go of her arm and ran his hand over her hair.

She stepped back, her hip bumping the counter.

"You had to do so much on your own. You can't know how I wanted to be here with you." He smiled again, and this time, his dimple flashed, and she searched his face, knowing that the anger was there, and the meanness, but he looked so charming. "You gotta know that you're the only one for me." He stepped closer and ran his hand over her cheek.

She stood her ground and suppressed a shiver. A shiver of revulsion.

"I know I had some problems, and you are always so patient and sweet with me. You always welcomed me back." The way he said "welcomed" made her want to wrinkle her nose, and it caused the back of her throat to close. "I want us to start over, baby. I want to do things right this time. I have a little place in Chicago, and I know you'll be comfortable there. We'll leave this behind, sell this diner, take the money, and build ourselves a whole new life."

A shot of fear went through her. The divorce settlement clearly said the diner was hers. He had gotten their pickup and several savings accounts.

They didn't actually own the building the diner was in, just the name and the business.

He couldn't take that from her. It was hers. It had been hers when they got married and was hers now.

She hoped she was right about that. But fear kept her mouth closed.

He moved forward more, until there was barely anything between them, and ran a hand down her arm. Maybe feeling emboldened by the fact that she hadn't moved back any more. She couldn't, since she was against the counter, but moving back meant retreat. She wasn't ready to do that.

"I know there's never been anyone for you but me, baby. I know I was your first kiss, your first boyfriend, your first...everything." His eyes glinted, and he didn't look handsome to her at that moment. "For the sake of our history together, let's try to salvage what we have and build it into something wonderful again."

She'd heard enough. She'd heard enough before he even opened his mouth.

She tried to put a pleasant smile on her face. Then she tilted her head ever so slightly. "No, thank you."

His eyes flashed, but he suppressed his anger. "I don't think that's what you really want. I think you miss me." His hands moved up her arms, and she did stretch away, leaning her torso back. He took a step forward, and he was closer than he was before, with his hand on her waist, and the other one on her cheek, rubbing over her forehead and down her temple.

"You're alone and lonely. I know you need me. I know you want me. And I promise, this time, it'll be us forever."

She almost rolled her eyes. That sounded like a line from some ridiculous movie, and she wanted to snort too.

"That's a very kind offer, but I'm not interested. Thanks. Now I've got some things I need to do."

She tried to push away, but he didn't move, until he did, and she realized that John had stepped forward and yanked him back.

She gave John a relieved and grateful look and moved quickly to the other side of the kitchen, putting the griddle between her and her ex.

The space made her bolder. That, and the fact that Danny had ignored her very polite no. "I don't think there's anything for you here. And you're wrong about me missing you."

"But you left all those messages for me. Every single day, it felt like you were calling me and leaving messages and begging me to come to you. I'm here now, baby."

"The messages were begging you to come see your son. And I left two. Two messages."

And yeah. She was probably begging. She never called Danny until Jordan cried which always tore her up.

"Fine," Danny said, shaking off John's hand which was still on his arm. "You'll be hearing from my lawyer. This diner is half mine, and you're gonna cough up the dough for it."

"I think it's a good idea to let our lawyers handle that. Because I'm pretty sure that the divorce settlement was final, and this is mine."

"We'll see about that."

He took another look at the men around him. If they hadn't been there, he might have gone after her again.

She wanted to think not. Even with all the arguments they had, he'd never hurt her, although he had gotten extremely angry at times.

She could keep herself under control during arguments. It was after they were over that she fell apart.

Danny gave her one last disgusted look, then he stalked out the door.

The tension that had strung her tight loosened, and she breathed out, turning to the people in the kitchen.

"I need to thank you. I need to thank you so much for more than just right now, but I can't do it now. I need to go sit down."

She felt like she could hardly catch her breath, and her words sounded short and airy. She turned, intending to go out the door and down the hall and up the stairs to her apartment.

But John's presence beside her stopped her.

"Are you okay?"

She stopped, wanting to lean into him. Wanting to take his strength, like he'd offered. Like he'd given her before.

She felt like she needed to do this on her own.

But then, she remembered what he said, about how in a perfect world, it was supposed to be two people. It was two people that became one, and they faced these things together.

She didn't have to be strong on her own, because she wasn't made to be strong on her own. She was made to be strong beside someone.

Unfortunately, the person that she was made to be strong beside had left, leaving her alone.

But that wasn't her fault. She wasn't even sure if it was his. Somehow, it was no longer unacceptable for a man to leave his wife, to fall in love with someone else, to decide that he didn't love her anymore. A spouse didn't really need a reason to just leave. Just because they wanted to was good enough.

It wasn't though. It wasn't a good enough reason to break a promise. To break a vow. To destroy a family and walk away from his responsibilities. It wasn't good enough.

She turned to John and laid her head on his chest. His arms came around her immediately, comforting and right. Her burden felt lighter immediately.

She felt like she could melt into him, and she stood there for a moment, her arms holding him tight, before she lifted her head. "If you don't mind, I think I do need to go lie down."

"I'll come check on you?"

She nodded, appreciating the concern that didn't cross the line into stifling or hovering. "Thank you." Her gaze caught on the other men who had begun to move, as well as Lindy and Iva May. "Thank you all. I wanted to come down this morning and thank everyone for the things that you've done for me, for putting in the time, and for helping me..."

"Please don't," Lindy said from the kitchen door where she still stood. "Don't worry about it. I know I wasn't here helping, at any point, because I felt like I had to come, and I don't resent a minute I've spent here. It made me feel good to be able to do something for you. Nothing needs to be said or done in return."

"I think she spoke for all of us when she said that. I know that's how I'm looking at the situation," Bill said. His voice was gruff, like he didn't want to get too emotional about it but was just letting her know. He shifted, like he felt constricted. "I hate to run away, but I know there are things out in the dining area that need to be taken care of. Take care of yourself, girl. That baby too."

Anitra's eyes widened, and she jerked her head up to John. "Did you—"

He shook his head, lifting his hands. "Not a word. Not to anyone, except the phone call I made to the OB/GYN."

"I think we kinda figured it out. Maybe someone came up with the idea, talked about it with the rest of us, and we decided we were right," Lindy said. "I don't remember who came up with the thought to begin with. Maybe me." She lifted her hands. "Probably me. It's a woman thing, I think."

"I knew, child. You know I did. But I didn't tell anyone. But if I figured it out, other people could too." Iva May's voice held nothing but concern and compassion.

She nodded. "I'm sorry. I didn't mean to look at anyone with accusations. Of course, you figured it out. I'm just the one who seems to be a million years behind everything."

"It's okay," Lindy said, coming forward and putting her hand on Anitra's back as Anitra turned and hugged her.

"Thank you for coming back. Thank you for standing with me. I appreciate it."

Lindy returned her hug, her arms strong and maternal. "Do you think he'll be back?"

Anitra shook her head. "He was always all talk. He's probably here because he already talked to the lawyer and found out there was nothing he could do. This is mine. And he can't take it. I don't know why he would try anyway. It's not really worth much."

"When someone needs money, even a little looks good," John said, and as Lindy stepped away, he drew close to her again, sliding his arm around her waist and easing her burden. It felt so right.

"Thank you."

"I'll see you in a bit."

She nodded.

Chapter 22

JOHN WATCHED AS ANITRA moved away. Iva May slipped in beside her, putting a steadying arm around her. They walked through the kitchen door, and he went back to the griddle.

He couldn't remember the last time he'd been that angry.

His body wasn't quite back under control, and the spatula shook in his hand.

"You good, man?" Adam asked, smacking a hand on his shoulder.

"Yeah. I'm fine."

"The guy's a jerk, but from what I understand, he's never been violent. He's also a big talker. I think Anitra will be okay."

"Yeah. Probably."

"I know you're a good thing for Anitra, and she must be pretty stuck on you, but I appreciate you giving her time. She's been through a good bit recently."

John nodded. Adam was a good man, and he appreciated him saying that John was good for Anitra. He also figured he could trust his judgment on her ex.

Adam walked off without saying anything more, and John grabbed an order after scraping the egg that had been burned off the griddle.

As had been the case the last week or so as they got deeper into the summer season, the morning rush had not really dissipated before it was time for John to leave.

He handed the spatula off to Bill, who was doing slightly better behind the griddle, and then went to look for Anitra after taking his apron off.

She stood at a table, talking, one hand on the small of her back, smiling. Looking for all the world like she hadn't had a serious confrontation with her ex just a couple of hours ago.

When she saw him, she put her hand up and said something more to the table before walking over to where he stood by the door.

"I know you don't have time, but I want to thank you," she said, and he shook his head.

"Not necessary. Will I see you tonight on the beach?"

She nodded.

"You'll text me if your ex shows back up?"

"You have enough to deal with at the hospital. I don't want to bother you."

"It's not a bother. I would consider it a favor." He tried not to plead, but Anitra's safety was more important to him than anything.

She nodded. "If he comes back, I'll text you."

"Thanks."

He walked out, not really wanting to, but he had his real job that he needed to go to.

Normally, he loved what he did, and he was even enjoying the transition time. Training new doctors, making sure all the systems and protocols were set up properly.

He had to admit he was looking forward to being done and cutting back his hours. Not just because of the books he wanted to write, but he wanted to be able to spend more time with Anitra. And hopefully their baby.

The day seemed to drag with more problems than usual. Finally, he was able to leave and went straight to the beach, getting there just before sunset.

He could have gone to Anitra's apartment, but he said they'd meet on the beach, and he felt like he needed to do that. Showing up at her apartment might be a little pushy.

Maybe she'd appreciate his concern. Because that's what it was, as he tried to keep from pacing back and forth.

Maybe he should have left a little earlier and gone for a jog. He'd already gone on one this morning, but his nervous energy felt like it needed an outlet.

Maybe Anitra felt the same, because he'd barely been there for five minutes when she walked on the beach.

He recognized the tunic dress immediately, despite the fact the beach, while not crowded, was busy. Strains from the band that played during the day on the weekend drifted down, although John barely heard it as he watched Anitra step out past the dunes.

She saw him immediately, and they walked toward each other.

"You're early," she said with a smile.

"So are you."

"Maybe I was looking forward to seeing you?"

"That might be why I was early too. And I wanted to make sure you were okay. I almost went to your apartment."

"That would have been fine. But the beach is nicer."

He almost wanted to talk to her about that. Could they speed up their timeline? He wanted to buy a place and settle down with her.

He was sure about that.

But he didn't want to rush her. Probably revisiting their "friendship" by the end of the summer was already rushing her.

Probably he should give her a year or more to adjust to her new life and make a decision about what she wanted.

He didn't want to wait that long.

Taking her hand, he asked, "Toward the pier?"

Her eyes shot to his, and then she nodded. They hadn't gone in the direction of the pier at all. Always the opposite direction.

He supposed it was time they faced that too.

"I wish there was a way we could check to see if your ex had left town."

"Adam said he thought he had. His car was parked at the gas station for a while, and Adam said that he talked to the landlord about renting, but it's summer, and there's nothing."

"Yeah. It does seem very busy."

"Yeah. Every house gets scooped up this time of year."

"Are you okay?"

"I am. I actually feel great. I wasn't sure I was ready to get out of the house, but I knew I needed to at least come down and thank everyone and see some customers again. It felt good to be around everyone and to see tourists I've known for years. I'm definitely ready to take my job back." She looked at him expectantly, like she was asking a question.

"I suppose I can give it back to you. Does that mean you don't want me to come anymore?" It wasn't that he enjoyed getting up so early in the morning. It wasn't even that he enjoyed cooking omelets, although he did enjoy the mindless work; it helped center his thoughts.

"Do you want to? I just assumed this was a huge drain on you. I hadn't even realized you were doing it..." Her voice trailed off, and he wasn't sure what the look on her face was. Not accusation. Betrayal?

"Are you upset that I didn't tell you?"

"I wondered why you'd kept it from me."

"I didn't really mean to. It just never seemed like a good time to tell you. I didn't want you to think that I was bragging or that I expected anything from you."

"It seemed like a lot for you to do on top of your actual job, which is hard and stressful."

"It's extra, sure. But there is a little bit of excitement in my morning every morning, when I walk into work and put the apron on." He stroked his fingers over her hand. "I wonder if today will be the day that I see you. Is that terrible?"

"And you never did," she said sadly.

"There are reasons for that. I understood. Now, there shouldn't be any reason why I wouldn't."

"No. I'll be down every day. But I usually work the griddle. What am I gonna do?"

"You can sit in the kitchen and talk to me."

She laughed. "I suppose I could spend more time with customers. We seem to be busier this year than we ever have before. Bill doesn't seem to mind waiting tables in the morning before he opens his shop, but maybe I should take his job."

"I'd rather see you than Bill's ugly mug."

"Bill is not ugly." She bumped his shoulder with hers, and he grinned.

"Are you telling me you think Bill is handsome?"

"I think so. Probably." Her eyes glinted up at him. "Not as handsome as you, if that's what you were wondering."

"I wasn't wondering any such thing," he said, which was a total lie.

"I see. You just want to know what I thought of Bill. His looks. Just for a conversation piece."

"Are you done teasing me?"

"I thought I was allowed to tease you."

"You are. Anytime. I enjoy it."

They walked by the pier in silence, although he wished he knew what she was thinking. There was a little bit of regret for him tied there. Mostly because of timing and that what they had done wasn't right.

Maybe a little astonishment, too. He still couldn't believe that he'd done what he did.

He'd never done anything like that before in his life. Not even close.

And yet, Anitra made him feel different, act different, and want different things than he ever had before.

He supposed that was what falling in love was like.

He also supposed he'd lived long enough to know that it wasn't just the feeling. Being with someone meant shifting everything in your life to not just make room for them, and accommodate them, but to live to give yourself to them, since the action of love itself was unselfish.

He wasn't sure if he was ready for that. He wanted to be.

It seemed to be an easy and natural thing to want to give more to Anitra. He almost felt like he could give up anything for her, and it wouldn't be a sacrifice. But more a labor of love.

New understanding of that phrase hit him, and he realized a labor of love really wasn't a labor at all. It was...enjoyable.

"I think you said I am welcome to stay at the diner for a couple of hours every morning?" he asked as the pier disappeared behind them.

"You most certainly are, but I do want to make sure that you don't work too hard. I think you should take several mornings off."

"If I take the mornings off, can I sit and watch you cook omelets?"

She laughed. "Isn't that defeating the purpose?"

"Taking off is defeating the purpose. The purpose is to come see you."

"Then come. But promise me you won't do more than what is healthy."

"I promise."

She turned her face up to smile at him, the orange glow of the sunset reflecting on her skin, and he hoped he got to do this—walk on the beach with Anitra—for the rest of his life.

Chapter 23

"I APPRECIATE YOU COMING with me," Anitra said as she patted the dirt around the flowers at the base of Jordan's tombstone.

"You know I wanted to," John said as he helped her to her feet.

She wasn't unwieldly, not yet, but she was getting there.

"I know you said you did, but..."

"I promise. I'm not going to tell you one thing and mean something different. I just won't."

She sighed. She had such a hard time believing that sometimes. Danny had been exactly the opposite. Typically, whatever he said, he had something else planned, or meant something else, or was just flat-out lying.

"Thank you for reminding me. Thank you for being patient with me while I try to believe you."

"You have to be patient with me about other things. I guess I owe you."

It wasn't true, but she didn't argue with him. She just reached over, and slipped her fingers in his, and smiled as he tightened his around hers and they looked down on Jordan's grave together.

"He would have been ten?"

She nodded. "He was born at 7:16 PM. The longest day of my life, I think." She laughed a little, remembering the pain.

It had faded, as it had for billions of women, when she held her baby in her arms.

John moved, checking his watch. "He's not quite here yet."

"Oh boy. Those last few minutes were the worst."

He pulled her toward him until she stood in front of him in what was his favorite pose. She enjoyed it too as he slipped his arms around her stomach and touched his cheek with hers.

"Just a couple minutes now."

"He weighed 8 lbs. 4 oz. and was 20 inches long."

"A chubby baby."

"Like his mother."

"I see that." His hand moved under her belly, and her face moved against his cheek, and they smiled.

"You seem mostly happy," he said. "I don't want to jinx anything, or dig up any bad memories, but just want to acknowledge that we've moved on."

"We have." Maybe not moved on exactly, but she was able to talk about Jordan without pain. Her head twisted, and the tips of their noses touched. "Mostly because of you."

"Don't give me more credit than I deserve. It took a lot of strength to go through what you did. And you did most of it by yourself."

He'd been with her when he could. At the diner, on the beach, on weekends, in the evenings. She would never doubt that his concern had been for her, first and foremost.

Finally, his schedule had slowed down some, and while the summer rush of tourists was not quite as heavy as it had been during its peak in July and the beginning of August, it was still quite busy.

"I had you. I had the Lord. Neither one of you ever left me. And I kinda think that you are sent by Him. I almost messed it all up, but I think He can take our mistakes and use it for good."

"I know He can."

They stood in silence for a little while, as the seconds ticked by, and then he looked at his watch. "And he's here. 7:16 PM on August 31."

"It's a boy," she said, remembering the doctor's words of so long ago and how they sent a pang through her of joy and love.

She was even more thrilled when he was declared healthy, and she heard the first cry, breathing on his own, angry at his abrupt entrance into the world.

"I wonder if he knows he's getting a sister?" John murmured with his cheek still next to hers.

"I think he did...." She wasn't sure how John would take this. "He'd told me once a while ago that Jesus told him he was getting a sister and that she could have his ball glove. He...he said she was going to love baseball, too. He never mentioned a brother or anything."

"I think we should believe him," John said, and she felt him smile beside her. He was always trying to do that—make her smile. "Maybe there will be another opportunity," he murmured, and her heart shivered.

She hoped he meant what she thought he did. He'd been going to the diner every morning, and since he was there to cook the omelets, she expanded her menu some, although they still closed at three.

He went to work, and she finished the day out in the diner, and they met on the beach in the evening, sometimes eating supper in her apartment before they left together.

Or he might take her out. But, for the most part, he kept his promise to be friends.

Maybe friends would split the cost of the meal, and he always picked it up, and he paid for her next three appointments.

He'd never hinted that before the baby came he might want her to be wearing his ring and on his insurance. He hadn't said anything like that to her, hadn't kissed her, hadn't done any more than hold their baby like he was doing now.

"Happy birthday, Jordan," he said.

She regretted, more than a little, that he hadn't gotten to know the son that she'd lost. She'd loved him so fiercely, and she wished he'd had the opportunity to love him too.

"Happy birthday, son," she echoed.

They stayed there for a while, each lost in their own thoughts, until she shivered and said, "Goodness. It's gotten chilly quickly now that the sun has gone down."

"Sure has. Do you want me to get you a sweater from the car?"

"Are you ready to go?"

He turned her to face him, holding both of her hands in his. "I am. But I wanted to ask you something."

Curious but not apprehensive, her eyes glowed as she looked at him.

"I have an appointment with the realtor this Saturday afternoon. I was hoping that maybe you could come with me? I have five different houses, and I need to whittle it down to three. Would you help with that?"

Her brows twitched when he asked his question. It wasn't something she was expecting.

"This is the last day of August," he stated.

She hadn't missed it. Her lips turned up. "You're never late."

"I wanted to be a lot earlier."

"I think I was ready earlier."

"Is that a yes?"

"It sure is."

Chapter 24

"THE VIEWS ARE GORGEOUS," Anitra said as she and John stood in front of the floor-to-ceiling windows in the great room. It had a cathedral ceiling, which made the windows even bigger and gave the impression of being open to the lake.

The house was on a bit of a bluff, so it would be protected from the worst of the winds and waves in the winter. "Do you think we would have a problem with that drop-off and the children?"

He grinned. "I've been to every appointment. I know there's only one." He spoke low, but there was a tease in his voice, and she grinned. Her cheeks reddened, and she looked away and down.

"With our daughter?" she corrected herself without looking at him.

He put a hand on her shoulder and used his thumb to stroke up her neck. She leaned into him, and he loved how she did that. It made him feel like she trusted him to protect her and take care of her, although he knew she was strong enough to stand on her own feet if she needed to.

He liked that she didn't. He liked that he didn't, either. Standing beside someone was much nicer than standing alone.

He would know about that, having spent his entire life alone.

"If we need to, we'll fence it. We'll do whatever it takes to keep her safe."

"We can go look at the grounds if you guys would like to," the realtor said, coming over with her folder pulled against her chest and a bright smile on her face.

John could have told her she didn't need to work too hard to sell this house. He was sold on it, unless Anitra liked one of the other two they'd already seen better.

"If you don't mind, I'd like to walk around one more time?" Anitra said, and John grinned. She couldn't see him, but it made him happy that she seemed to really like it.

"Of course. Take your time."

The previous owners had already moved out, so there was no furniture or pictures. Nothing but walls and carpet.

He supposed Anitra, with her eye for design, would be able to picture it with her style and décor.

"I think this will be pretty cozy on a winter day."

"I agree. I love those big windows."

They held hands as they walked off to the side and down the hall where the study was on one side. Farther down was the master bedroom.

Anitra wandered through the rooms again, and he went along for the ride. He did not need to see it again to know that this was the house that he wanted, although either of the other two would work as well, whatever Anitra wanted.

After they'd toured the other bedrooms, along with the great room which included the kitchen and the dining room as well as the huge living room, and the loft upstairs, along with another large room, they stepped outside as the realtor locked it behind them.

"What do you think?" he asked low as they walked down the path and around the house to the front.

"My favorite by far."

"Me too." He grinned. Somehow, he could just tell by looking at her that she liked this house the best. Her face was more animated and her eyes brighter. "I think the realtors do that on purpose. Save the best for last."

"Maybe they do. It's probably the most expensive too?"

He nodded. "Well within what we can afford."

Her eyes twitched a little when he said "we."

She questioned him. "We?"

"I guess I've been thinking about us that way a lot."

"I try not to, because it seems like such a dream."

"Would it continue to be a dream if I ask you to go to Boston to meet my parents?"

"Oh my goodness."

"If you're surprised that I'm serious, you shouldn't be."

"No. I guess not. I just...I just feel like it's a dream."

"So do you think you could sleepwalk to Boston?"

"Very funny," she said with a laugh. "I'm sure I can manage to sleep my way to Boston or wherever else you want to go."

"Boston is it. My parents are there, and I think if I go for a visit, my sister might come in too. You can meet them all at the same time."

"Your parents and a sister?"

He nodded. "I wanted to fly before it got too uncomfortable for you."

His eyes dropped to her stomach, and she nodded. "Will they have a problem with that?"

"I think they'll be thrilled I found someone who will put up with me. Finally."

"It wasn't hard. There are plenty of women who would be honored to have you."

"Well, they managed to trip over themselves to the point where I couldn't see them, I guess. Which makes me very happy right now, since that means I got the best."

She smiled, then her eyes looked around the yard. "They actually do have a fence, I hadn't seen it from the window, and I think this is the one I like the best." She tilted her head. "You too?"

"Definitely."

The realtor made it around to where they stood and rattled off some of the highlights of the exterior of the home.

They listened in silence, and then when she was done, John said, "I think we've seen enough. We'll go home and think about it, and I'll let you know what we decide."

They'd already made a decision, but he felt like maybe they should sleep on it before they announced it and decided to make an offer.

He said as much to Anitra on their drive back down. It wasn't far from Blueberry Beach, just a little north.

"I think that's smart. I'm sure I know what I want, but sometimes you lie in bed at night and think of all the things you didn't think of during the day."

"Exactly. I don't want to end up making a mistake. I want to make the right decision the first time."

"I guess I can say here that it doesn't matter to me where we live. We don't have to pick any of the houses that you chose. I'm happy in my apartment, as long as you're there."

"I am too. I guess that means I have one more thing I'd like to ask you."

"Yes?" she asked, looking at him inquiringly.

"Do you have a few more minutes?"

"I'm yours until tomorrow morning at the diner."

"All right then." He drove a few more miles, taking the exit for the Blueberry Beach.

He parked and got out.

He knew she didn't understand, but she got out as well and took his hand when he offered it.

He took his shoes and socks off. She did the same, shooting him a confused glance, and they walked out on the beach, perfect timing as the sun was setting.

When he made it to the pier, he reached into his pocket and dropped to a knee. Maybe someone else would have all the pretty words, but he spoke what was in his heart.

"I love you. Would you marry me?"

She smiled and then laughed, putting a hand up to cover her face before she took it down, and said, "Yes! Yes!"

He took the ring out of the box and slid it on her finger, saying, "If you don't like it—"

"It's perfect."

"I didn't do anything fancier because you don't seem to like fancy, but if you're sure?"

"I am. I wasn't expecting this."

"What? Did you think we'd just go move in together?"

"I don't know. Lots of people do that. I guess. Yes. No. I don't know!"

"Sorry. I never meant to give any impression other than my intention to marry you. I'm sorry if you had even a moment's doubt about that. That's all my fault. I should have done better."

"No. If I had questions, I could have asked. You've been patient with me, with everyone. I've never seen you angry."

"I was angry when your ex showed up in the diner."

"I couldn't tell."

"I'm trained as a healer. I've taken an oath to do no harm. I really wanted to do some harm that day."

"You didn't, and he's gone."

"Are you sure?"

"I think so. My mom said he's on Facebook and he's with someone else. Or maybe he ditched her and is with someone else. I don't know. I don't care, as long as he's leaving me alone. My lawyer has assured me over and over that he might inquire and he can if he wants to, but the agreement is settled, and there's nothing more to talk about."

"That's right. It's good to hear."

"For me, too."

"I know this area is not our best. For self-control anyway. But I wanted to kiss you. That's it. Just kiss you."

"I want you to."

He bent his head, his lips touching hers, familiar yet new. As soft as he remembered.

Her hands went around his neck, and he pulled her close, not quite as slender as she had been earlier in the year. It didn't matter. He loved the person inside the body. He loved the way they just seemed to fit together, their personalities fit and his spirit seemed destined to be with hers.

She made a sound, and his hands tightened, and he deepened the kiss, his heart beating so loudly it drowned out the waves.

He wanted this. Along with the friendship and the companionship and the laughter and the fun and the baby between them. He wanted this, too. This made everything complete.

He lifted his head, not that he wanted to, but he needed to. He didn't want any repeats. Not now anyway.

"I love you," she whispered, the words sweet music to his ears.

"How soon?" His closed eyes opened as her lips tilted up.

"Tomorrow?"

"Don't you need longer than that to plan a wedding?"

"Oh. You'll be disappointed if we don't have a big wedding?"

He snorted. "Hardly."

"Then why have it?"

"Don't you want it?"

She shook her head. "Not even a little."

"Then tomorrow it is."

"Are you serious?"

"Now the lady has changed her mind?"

"No. She's just really shocked that the man is agreeing with her. For once."

"Oh, that was unnecessary. I always agree with you."

"I hardly think we can say always."

"Details."

"Speaking of, we'll need a preacher. A license."

"There might be a waiting period. I'll have to look."

"In that case, we'd better plan for later this week."

"The sooner, the better."

"I have to agree with that."

"See? We do agree."

"One kiss is not enough."

"Agreed."

So, he lowered his head and kissed her again.

THANK YOU SO MUCH FOR reading! There are more books in the Blueberry Beach series. You can see them HERE[1].

I'd love to see you in my Reader Chat.[2]

If you'd like to keep up to date with me and my writing and life, sign up for my newsletter[3]!

---

1. https://www.amazon.com/gp/product/B08RW8K6XC
2. https://www.facebook.com/groups/jessiegussman
3. https://dl.bookfunnel.com/f5u4jxd8r8

Made in the USA
Las Vegas, NV
30 July 2023